A Strange Enchantment

SHROPSHIRE GARDEN

I found warm silence in a Shropshire garden,
And through the long September days I dreamed,
While peaches ripened on the mellow walls,
And flowers of autumn gleamed,
Pungent and cool; the red apples hung
Like small suns in the green foliage,
And no songs were sung
On the misty mornings,
Purple-tinted with the stars of Michaelmas.

In that sunny, tranquil place
I was content, seeing through the brightening trees
The old, quiet house, delighting with its grace
My hungry eyes, and with its silence
My weary mind.

1941. Wilcot Hall, Shropshire.

From The Haunted Valley *and Other Poems by Mabel Esther Allan. Merseyside:*
Charles Gill & Son (Printers) Limited, 1981

A Strange Enchantment

Mabel Esther Allan

Dodd, Mead & Company · New York

1 2 3 4 5 6 7 8 9 10

Library of Congress Cataloging in Publication Data

Allan, Mabel Esther.
A strange enchantment.

Summary: Sixteen-year-old Prim becomes a farm
laborer during World War II in England and finds the
life very agreeable.
[1. Great Britain—History—20th century—Fiction.
2. World War, 1939–1945—Great Britain—Fiction]
I. Title.
PZ7.A4Sp   [Fic]   82-5049
ISBN 0-396-08044-8   AACR2

*Birth was a faraway thing to me, only half understood. But little
animals were charming. I had thought of feeding lambs from a bottle
but not of lambs being born. In town you are distant from such
things.*

*"I'll learn," I said, and I was to remember those two words. In-
deed I learned, through cold and misery and sometimes a strange
enchantment.*

Contents

I Join the Land Army

"Do you mind if I leave school and join the Land Army?" I asked my mother, on the day after war was declared.

It was early September and a lovely morning. Outside, in our town garden, the goldenrod was just opening into full flower. I had sat staring at it the morning before, Sunday, as we all listened to the Prime Minister's broadcast, telling us that we were at war with Germany.

I had felt excitement coupled with fear as I listened to that voice telling us we were facing a new kind of life. Nothing was going to be the same, so I couldn't just stay on at school. During the months when war had seemed to be inevitable I had fastened on the idea of going farming. Women had done it in the other war, before I was born. I always longed for the country and was restless in town; such a big town, Wallasey on the River Mersey.

We might, of course, all be going to die quite soon, but if not. . . . I interrupted our peaceful breakfast with my abrupt question, and Mother put down the teapot, staring at me, wide eyed.

"Join the Land Army, Prim? You're only sixteen; not seventeen until the end of January. They wouldn't have you."

"I could stretch it a bit," I said. "A little lie would be justified, don't you think? Everyone will be joining something. I'm nearly grown up, and strong."

"You'd need to be," my brother Charles remarked. He looked amused, which was annoying. He was eighteen, and was to be a medical student in Liverpool in a few weeks' time. "Of course you are *big*." He sketched a very unflattering shape of me with his hands. "They'd believe you if you said you were eighteen, in spite of that baby face."

"Oh, shut up, Charles!" I said. "I'm serious."

"Then if Prim's going to be a female farm laborer, I'll enlist for the Air Force," said Charles.

Mother's face was grave and I felt suddenly guilty. She only had us, for our father, who had been a doctor, had died nearly three years before. Mother had gone back to teaching and was English and History mistress at my school, St. Helen's. It was the biggest private school in the town. Both Charlie and I had been brought up to be independent and sensible, and she wasn't at all possessive; rather the other way, curiously objective about us.

Yet, in this strange world of war, perhaps I ought to consider her. And I adored Charlie, in spite of his annoying ways. He was the one who might die quickest, if he joined up, though of course there would be air raids. The sirens had sounded within a few hours of war being declared, but it had turned out to be a false alarm. Chilling, though, to hear that frightful rising and falling wail.

"Charles," said Mother, "you'll go to the university and stay there as long as you're allowed. You're not like Prim; you know what you want to be. You must get in some studying before they call you up. Maybe the war will be over in a few months."

"Oh, I hope not!" Charles exclaimed. "I do want to be a doctor, but I wouldn't mind a few adventures first."

"If you call *war* an adventure . . ."

"Well, it is, in a way, to the male sex."

"Oh, do shut up, Charles!" I shouted. "Mother's right. You ought to get your foot into the university; then they'll have to take you back. And I know perfectly well what I want to do in a year or two, when the war's over. I want to go to an art school. But I can't just stay on at an ordinary school *now*. I've always longed to live in the country, so I would like to join the Land Army."

Mother sat in silence, looking at us both. I learned much later that she was thinking that Merseyside would be a target for the enemy, since Liverpool was such an important port. I was too old to be evacuated, and I would be safe in the country, on some remote farm. It never occurred to me that I might get out of a danger area by joining the Land Army. If it had, I believe I would have thought of something else.

"Prim," Mother said at last, "you may go and register

for the Land Army, if that's really what you want. I think it will be a very hard life. You know nothing about how the country is run. You just see lambs in fields, and men harvesting oats and wheat. Have you thought that winter's coming? A wartime winter. You may have to get up before six to start milking."

It must be rather pleasant in a warm cowshed, I thought. I had an idea that cows had sweet breath, and the milk, frothing and foaming, would pour rhythmically into buckets. And there might be tiny lambs to feed with a bottle and, when spring came with hawthorn covering the hedgerows, I would wander around feeding ducks and doing other pleasant tasks in the sun.

"May I go this morning, then? I think you register at the Assembly Rooms. There were notices up when I passed yesterday."

"Yes, go. But if they haven't sent for you by the time school starts you must go on with your classes."

"Oh, I'll be helping with the harvest," I said gaily.

Charles laughed even more annoyingly than usual.

"My poor Primrose! The harvest is probably in already. It's September and the weather's been good. Don't you remember, when we were out in the car weeks ago, there were carts laden with oats and wheat. Barley, too."

I was silent, not wishing to admit I didn't know the difference. My vision of country life was a wholly romantic one, born of holidays and short journeys in our old car. Charles certainly knew more, because his great friend, Bill Wainwright, had an uncle who owned a farm out in Cheshire, and they had both stayed there and helped in the fields sometimes. I had often angled for an invitation, but Bill just laughed and said, "It's not for girls. The work would be too hard for you, Prim."

Now was my chance to show Bill that he was wrong. Maybe he'd notice me more when I came home from the country a fully fledged worker. But it wasn't only that. I wanted to join the Land Army more than I had ever wanted anything in my life; my *dull* life. War was frightening, but it gave me my chance to go adventuring.

I went upstairs to get ready to go out. I must look as old as possible, but not too "towny." In the holidays I often wore shorts or slacks, depending on the weather. I had some very nice shorts; gray, with pleats. I took off the old pink dress that I had put on because my friend Kathleen had said we might go to the outdoor swimming pool, if it was open on that second day of war. Swimming now seemed unimportant, even wrong.

The shorts, and a thin white blouse, and my blue necklace at the open neck. We were not allowed to use make-up in school, but I had two lipsticks. I stared at myself in the glass and thought I might easily pass for eighteen. I gave my dark brown hair, that I wore rather long, a brief flick with a comb, and went downstairs again. I said "Wish me luck!" and walked out into the hot street. I felt like a crusader going to the wars as I headed down Manor Road.

Somehow I expected the world to look different, but

it didn't; not my bit of it, anyway. Traffic was roaring along as usual, and the only thing that was not the same was that so few children played in the side streets. A great many had been evacuated on Friday.

The Assembly Rooms had been familiar to me all my life. I went to my first dancing class in the ballroom when I was five. A few people were coming and going, and a woman was sitting at a table in the gloomy entrance hall. I told her, "I want to join the Women's Land Army, please."

"In there," she said, waving her hand, and I entered a small, dim room where two other women were sitting at a table, surrounded by notices and with piles of forms in front of them. The one with white hair, who was drinking tea and looking bored, greeted my request without surprise and gave me a form.

I filled it in over at another table by the wall. I moved my age up a year (it *must* be justified) and added other details: "Primrose Rachel Harvey, The Hollies, Manor Road, Wallasey, Cheshire." Over Occupation I hesitated, then filled in "Unemployed." When I took the form back the woman glanced at it and said, "Unemployed! Can't you get a job, dear?"

"I . . . I haven't really looked. I left school quite recently."

"You do know that farming is a hard life? Long hours and poor pay. Some farmers are unwilling to pay overtime, we've heard."

"Yes, I know it's hard. I don't mind about overtime."

"Well, you'll be hearing from the county office in Chester."

So it was done, and I went out into the sunshine feeling weak and slightly sick. It wouldn't take long; they would send for me next week, or the week after. I was scared, but elated.

They did not send for me next week or the week after. School opened and I went back to my classes. Mother paid a term's fees in advance, which made me feel guilty, but she explained to the headmistress, Miss Barlow, that I might have to leave suddenly.

St. Helen's seemed different that September. It was partly because I was restless and impatient to be gone, and also because many of the younger girls had been evacuated.

Another month passed and there was still no word from Chester. I felt more and more unsettled and out of step with everyone. Kathleen was annoyed with me because I had joined the Land Army and she said I wouldn't stick farm life for a week. Bill was often at our house and he teased me unmercifully. "What, Prim, not slaving yet? Alas, you see your fair hands aren't needed for the war effort. You'll loathe it, you know."

"I will *not* loathe it. I can work as hard as anyone."

"You haven't tried," Bill said heartlessly. He was at Liverpool University, too, and had turned even more lordly than Charles. It infuriated me that he persisted in treating me as a schoolgirl.

13

Christmas came, that first Christmas of the war. The weather was lovely on Christmas Day, and Mother, Charlie, and I went to the beach at Harrison Drive and walked for miles along the sand. There was a heavenly sunset and it was hard to believe in war.

But darkness came early, and next day it was very cold. By then I had almost forgotten about farming and was resigned to another term at school. The thought of the Land Army had lost most of its charm in the dark of winter. On the day after Christmas I lay curled up on my bed in my own lovely room and read a new novel. My room was warm because of the electric fire, and all my books were there and the pictures I had chosen myself over several birthdays and Christmases. They were mostly reproductions of French Impressionists, but there were also several pencil drawings by me.

Such a peaceful, happy day. Next morning before it was light the post came, the first since Christmas Day, when there had only been cards. And then my heart leaped sickeningly, for there was a long, thin brown envelope from the Women's Land Army county office in Chester. I shouted "It's come!" and tore open the envelope. It contained a form with certain words filled in. I was to be at the county office at 3:00 P.M. on Friday, December 29, for an interview.

By Friday it was bitterly cold and snowing slightly. I felt shivery and strange as I sat in the unheated bus, and even more cold and uncertain as I waited with four other girls in a drafty passage. Three of them were sneezing and coughing. The one without a cold was small and thin, and she wore a tweed coat and a pointed hood of the same material. She sat tensely, gazing at the blank wall opposite. She had big brown eyes and a pretty mouth, but she looked like a sick elf. So pale and cold.

They were all older than I was, even the thin elf. The only one who seemed disposed to talk, in spite of her cold, had lovely fair hair under a little fur hood, and gentle blue eyes. She was twenty-three, she said, and lived in the country already. She had never had a job, but she thought the Land Army would be fun. Her voice, though husky with cold, had an assertive briskness that went oddly with her gentle look. A privileged girl, wearing expensive clothes. Hard to imagine her as a low-paid farm worker. She drew from the sick elf that her name was Jane Preston, that she was eighteen and a half, and in service, and from the other two that they both worked in the same factory near Crewe.

Before she could question me she was called in first, and we sat in silence. I slid my drawing pad and pencil from my shoulder bag and was soon absorbed in a picture of Jane Preston.

The first girl came out after about five minutes, said, "I'm to go to Westringham College!" and departed. Then my name was called. I bundled pad and pencil back into my bag and walked, quaking, into the interview room where several women were seated around a large polished table. They didn't look as if they would know much about the country. They were all smartly dressed and looked like town types.

I stood at the foot of the table, like a naughty school-girl. They asked a few questions, such as: "Do you like the country?" "Do you know that farming is hard work?" "Are you prepared to go anywhere in England when your training is finished?" I answered "Yes" to all of them, and they consulted together in low voices. I heard one woman say, "Not quite eighteen, but she looks strong. And when spring comes there'll be a big demand."

What would they say if they knew I was only sixteen? But I just had to be accepted, because everyone would laugh if I were turned down. Winter and snow. . . . Who cared?

The woman nearest me, wearing a beautiful fur coat, turned to me and said, "I hope, Miss Harvey, you aren't like the girl who said she would like to learn to milk but would prefer to begin on a calf?"

A calf? In another moment I saw that it was a joke and I laughed. Everyone laughed and the interview was over. A paper was pushed toward me and I was asked to sign.

"You may go to Westringham College next Wednesday. They've given the men's quarters over to the Land Army, and the peacetime students are gradually leaving. There you'll learn every aspect of general farming This is your railway voucher and you will be given your uniform on arrival. You'll need to take a doctor's certificate with you. After your training, which may last from five to eight weeks, you will be sent to a farm."

I stumbled out, passing Jane Preston in the doorway.

"It's not alarming," I whispered. "Rather silly, really. I don't believe they know a thing about farming, but I'm to go to Westringham on Wednesday."

Outdoors it was already dark and the snow was falling faster. The streets were slushy and the cathedral was almost invisible through the drifting flakes. I had got what I wanted, but . . .

"Oh, what have I *done*?" I asked myself.

The Way to Westringham College

The snow stopped, but the weather was cold, wet, and dark. On New Year's Day it was announced by Royal Proclamation that all males between the ages of nineteen and twenty-eight would be called up for service in the Armed Forces. My heart quailed when I looked at Charlie, and Mother's lips pinched. He wouldn't be nineteen for some months, but it brought the war horribly nearer.

"By spring we'll really know there is a war," said Charlie.

If there hadn't been a war I would have been at school for another year and a half, and not bound for Westringham Agricultural College on Wednesday. As the hours passed, home seemed infinitely desirable and comfortable, and for the first time I really thought about living with strange people on some remote farm. But it was too late to be cowardly, and I put as brave a face on it as I could. I had everything to learn, but, in my brash and awful ignorance, I was really quite unaware of the fact and just rather scared of the step into the unknown at that gloomy time of year. In the blacked-out streets of wartime Wallasey, the country seemed very remote.

On my last evening Mother came into my room and sat on the edge of my bed. Her gaze went to the new pencil sketch I had just fastened to the door with drawing pins. "That's rather good," she said. "Who is it?"

"Jane Preston," I told her. "I did the rough while we were waiting to be interviewed. I wonder if she was accepted. Can you imagine her going farming?"

"No," Mother admitted. "But there was a bit in the *Daily Mail* this morning about the girls from different walks of life who are joining the Land Army. I suppose it will be interesting."

I thought of the girl in the fur hood, with the assured voice and the contrasting gentle blue eyes, and the two from Crewe.

"I'll be one of them, but they'll all be grown up," I said.

"You're grown up now, Prim," Mother replied, a little sadly. "I can only trust you to have good sense. I don't think we can really imagine what it will be like on a small farm in winter. You may have to do all kinds of unpleasant things, and meet people who aren't very pleasant, too. Cows have calves and pigs have . . . litters, is it? You may have to help. Have you thought of that?"

I hadn't, actually. Birth was a faraway thing to me, only half understood. But little animals were charming.

I had thought of feeding lambs from a bottle but not of lambs being born. In town you are distant from such things.

"I'll learn," I said, and I was to remember those two words. Indeed I learned, through cold and misery and sometimes a strange enchantment.

Mother had bought me a new coat at the beginning of winter, and I chose a thick dark green one, thinking it would be right for the Land Army. So, when I set off on Wednesday morning, I was wearing that coat, a green cap, and strong shoes. At least I thought they were strong until I saw the pair issued by the Land Army.

Mother drove me over the docks to Woodside Station, Birkenhead. As we bumped over the bridges in the gray, cold light she said, "I suppose the poor old car will soon be no use to us. There'll be petrol rationing."

The train was pretty full, with suitcases and kit bags on top of my luggage in the rack. There were young soldiers, a party of nuns, and several girls wearing the smart uniform of the Wrens. In a few hours I would be in uniform, too. I shivered with excitement and cold; the train was unheated.

I had to change at Chester General and my suitcase seemed very heavy as I lugged it over the bridge. Westringham College was in the same county but at the southern end of it, and it was an awkward journey. I had to change again at Crewe, then travel a short distance on a third train. My instructions were to leave my luggage at the station and walk to the college.

The Crewe train was going on to London and was packed. As we roared through the Cheshire countryside, I sat on my suitcase in the corridor. Suddenly someone poked her head out of the nearest compartment and I recognized Jane Preston . . . little pale face, big brown eyes, and wisps of dark hair under the pointed hood.

"Hello!" I cried. "We met before. Are you going to Westringham, too?"

"Yes." She came out to join me and someone immediately took her seat. It didn't matter, for we'd soon be in Crewe. "I'm so glad to meet you! Are you scared? I'm just terrified."

"It'll be all right when we get there, I suppose." I wasn't ready to admit how scared I was. "There'll be others in the same boat. But I don't know a thing about farming."

"Neither do I. But it was something they said I could do, because it meant living with a family. I'm an orphan and I was at a home in Chester; then they put me into service. But I didn't like it, and I wanted to do *something* to help the war. I've always longed for the country, only somehow I didn't expect to start in midwinter. I put down my name back in September."

"Just like me," I said wryly. "It did seem different then. But, never mind, it'll be an adventure." She didn't look as if she would enjoy adventures, but her face was very determined.

"I've got to stick it and do well," she said.

Crewe Station was huge, echoing, and bitterly cold. Already the afternoon was turning dark and misty, and the mist wreathed under the high arched roof. A voice over the loud-speaker said that the Westringham train would depart in five minutes. Panting, we hurried to the platform and flung ourselves and our suitcases into a blessedly almost empty compartment. It was just a little local train, very shabby and rather dirty.

The only other passenger, a woman in a fur coat and high boots, put out a thin hand and lifted my label. "Oh, no!" she cried, in a deep voice. "I see you're going to Westringham, too. Do they take babies, then, in the Land Army?"

"I'm not a baby!" I answered, annoyed. She had a thin face with good features and hazel eyes, and she looked quite old. I learned later that she was thirty-five. She was one of the oldest at the college.

"Well, you look it, dear, though you're probably a good deal stronger than I am. I wouldn't have said the other one was the type."

Jane, clearly demoralized by the cool, drawling voice and the searching gaze, sat down and shrank into her corner. I found the stranger off-putting, too, but . . . "Are *you* the type?" I asked boldly. I reminded myself that I was grown up and on an equal footing with everyone else.

She laughed. "Heaven knows, little one. Only time will tell. I felt that agriculture was one of the things that might survive the war, and, if it's to be a case of the survival of the fittest, I thought I'd land myself in the right place. It's going to be grim, though. A crowd of women huddled together in this weather."

I was used to "a crowd of women," so I hadn't thought of it that way, but she was clearly very sophisticated. As the train steamed across the darkening fields, she told us that she came from Shrewsbury, but had lived in London and other places. She had done some acting, published a novel—a pretty poor novel, she said—been a journalist, and driven all over Britain helping with some kind of survey. Her name was Hilary Buckden.

By the time she had finished telling us we were drawing into Westringham. It was almost dark and the mist was thick. The stationmaster, holding a dim, shielded lantern, told us to put our suitcases in the ticket office. "They'll come for them in one of their lorries. See, there are several already. I'm sorry for you young ladies having that two-mile walk. Turn left when you leave the station yard. The college gates are on the left side of the road."

"Thanks," Hilary said, and slipped a coin into his hand. "What a rotten do!" she grumbled, when we were on the road. "Come on, children. Step it out. At least it'll make a good chapter one day, or a newspaper article."

"Do you write about everything that happens to you?" I asked, and she laughed and said, "Some of it."

It was a horrible walk, for there was quite a lot of traffic, and we had to walk on the muddy and wet grass verge.

"How old are you children?" Hilary asked, after we had walked for some time in a silence broken only by her muttered curses. The whole Land Army had been consigned to hell because no transport had been provided for us.

As I didn't answer, Jane said, "Eighteen." I muttered, "I'll be eighteen before the end of the month." I felt awful, lying.

"You could have fooled me," Hilary said and put her arm carelessly around my shoulders. My heart sank. I was in for trouble if the instructors were as observant as she was.

"I don't see why," I said, finding that careless arm rather an alarming comfort. I had never met anyone like her before, but then it was obvious that I was in for many shocks. I was growing aware that my world had been a very narrow one.

"Well, tell me all about your lives, children dear," she said. She released me to walk behind, as a large truck skimmed past her. She cursed vividly again as it disappeared.

There wasn't much I could tell safely. Even Charlie's age was a problem now *I* was older. Jane said unexpectedly, "She draws, Primrose does. She was drawing while we were waiting to be interviewed the other day."

24

I hadn't realized she had noticed.

"One day I hope to go to a good art school," I said.

"Clever child!" Hilary cried. "That's something I can't do. Dear Heaven! How far have we gone, do you think? And what do you do, Jane?"

"Nothing clever," Jane said. "I was brought up in an orphanage because my parents were killed in an accident when I was nine. I thought . . . I like animals, or I *think* I do."

"It won't all be chickens and piglets," Hilary remarked. "I hope you like bulls. A girl I know slightly who was here in the last batch had to take a bull for a walk. Yes, really. Some kind of test. She had to put a short pole through the ring in his nose and walk him half a mile before daylight."

"You're joking," I said uncertainly.

"No, sweet Primrose, I am not. Fact. They had to kill hens by twisting their necks. One girl fainted and another was sick. You may as well know what you're in for."

"I wouldn't faint, I'd die," said Jane.

We walked on and on. By then it was quite dark, and the mist wreathed in our faces, clammy and cold. I wondered wildly if I should go back to the station and take the next train home. While I was wondering, I slipped off the grass verge and there was a loud hooting close behind me, and dim lights. A large vehicle drew up and a man's voice yelled, "Do you want to get killed? Fool women! No sense!"

"There are other people in the world without sense,"

Hilary drawled. "The fools who expected us to walk from the station."

"Oh, you're some of our lot. I might have known. Get in among the luggage and be quick about it."

"And no manners, either," Hilary said, as she swung herself up into the lorry. Jane and I followed. In about three minutes we passed through open gates and seemed to be driving up a long, tree-arched avenue. The lorry crunched onto gravel and a huge house loomed up dimly above us.

The driver got down and said, "Well, here we are! Help to carry the stuff in, will you? I must get to milking."

My fingers were so cold I could hardly grasp the handle of the first suitcase he handed down, but I staggered with it through a great door and found myself in a large hall. It was cold, and rather gloomy, and in a way very impressive. There was a lot of heavy furniture, and a wide staircase, embellished with carvings, branched under a portrait of a man in Victorian clothes. Just descending the lower part of the staircase was a woman wearing a smart black dress. She greeted me without enthusiasm.

"Ah, another of our girls? Oh, and two more. And the luggage. Thank you, Mr. Blane."

"That's the lot," Mr. Blane said. I had my first look at him, and was surprised to find that he was quite young and not bad looking. Dark eyes and hair and interesting bones. But I had taken an instant dislike to

26

that voice out of the mist, and I hoped he wasn't going to instruct me in the art of milking. Yet his voice, though so irritable, had an unfamiliar and attractive tone. There was a faint lilt that didn't quite seem to be Welsh.

The woman in black was Mrs. Varley, the lady warden of the college. She led us to her office, asked our names, and ticked them off on a list. Then she led us upstairs, telling us that, in future, we were to use the back staircase. The main staircase was strictly forbidden.

"Dear God!" Hilary muttered. "The Golden Staircase! Did you know you were coming to boarding school, Primrose?"

I was too overawed and scared to answer. The lady warden led us into a large, ice-cold bedroom not far from the top of the stairs and said, "You three will share this room. You will be expected to keep it tidy. The rules of the college will be read out this evening, then pinned on the notice board in the entrance hall. You will also be given your uniforms. You are the second batch of girls we've had. I hope you prove satisfactory." And she went away briskly.

"What a welcome when we only want to serve our country," said Hilary. "Well, if you children are going to sleep with me, I hope we get on together. Not too much girlish giggling, please."

I had never felt further from giggling in my life. I felt cold all through and simply appalled. All my dreams were in the dust; not that there was any. The room was clinically bare and clean. Little animals . . . summer fields . . . walking through barley . . . picking apples. Those things seemed a world away from that Victorian mansion in the Cheshire fields, not far from the Shropshire border.

Jane sat on the nearest bed, and Hilary winced as it creaked. The face of the sick elf in the pointed hood stared at me in dismay, and I stared hopelessly back.

If only I'd had a room to myself I wouldn't have minded so much. But I was stuck with Jane and the terrifying Hilary, and there was nothing to be done about it.

Hilary, Jane, and Mr. Blane

We had barely started our unpacking when a gong
sounded loudly below. Hilary said, "Thank God! Food,
little ones! Run!"

"But we haven't even washed our hands. Where's the
bathroom?" I asked, in a panic. I was weak with hunger, but very conscious that I couldn't be looking my
best after the journey.

"There's a place with wash basins next door," Hilary
said coolly. "Baths, if they exist, are somewhere else. If
you must wash, kiddies, be quick about it."

But she snatched up her toilet bag and came with us.
We hastily washed our hands, and Hilary put on some
very bright lipstick. I couldn't find mine.

We went down the back stairs and followed others
into the dining room. It was a large room, with a dec-
orated ceiling supported by pillars, yet there was absolutely nothing in it but long tables covered with oilcloth
and rows of wooden benches. It was bitterly cold, and
the little groups of girls and women who were drifting
in looked pinched and unhappy. Several of them were

coughing and one was sneezing violently. Hilary said, "I was wrong, Primrose. It isn't a boarding school, it's a sanatorium." And suddenly her bored, deep voice seemed to me irresistibly funny. I laughed out loud, and all heads turned in my direction. Hilary said approvingly, "That's better! I abhor giggling children, but I'm relieved that you find me amusing."

"Yes, I do," I said boldly. Amusing, but still terrifying. Those hazel eyes were taking in everything. She had a kind of elegance, too, though she was wearing old slacks and two old sweaters. She was very slim and she moved like a dancer, but she wasn't good looking, really. Interesting in a bony way, though.

Hilary, Jane, and I sat together. I counted and there were twenty-five of us. Apart from myself and Jane, they all looked over twenty. The two from Crewe didn't seem to be there, but the girl who had worn the fur hood was at the end of our table. Opposite us were four girls who were all pale, with blonde hair. They could have been sisters, but we soon learned that they didn't even know each other. One came from London, one from Bristol, and two from Birmingham. Hilary had soon named them collectively as "the Blondes."

The girl who had worn the fur hood had a cloud of golden hair and her eyes looked bluer than before. She was soon telling everyone in her high, clear, upper-class voice that she lived in Staffordshire "in a big country house, you know, and I'm keen on horses. Daddy said everyone had to do their bit and the Land Army would be nicest for me."

"Hope she thinks so in a few weeks' time," murmured Hilary. "Those misty blue eyes were meant to smile over the hunting field. They'll cut no ice at six in the morning, unless she can charm Mr. Blane." After that she always called Althea Blayden-Shaw "Misty," and the name stuck.

The food was served through a hatch and was hot and quite good. I felt better after vegetable soup and omelettes, followed by custard and stewed apples.

We found our way to the common room, which was long and narrow, with an open fire awkwardly placed in a corner. We were called away in small groups to get our uniforms. Hilary, Jane, and I were called together.

We were taken down into an incredibly cold basement room, and someone called Miss Potter doled out all the things we would need. I found myself the possessor of a heavy brown raincoat, two khaki working smocks, two ribbed woolen sweaters in a nice dark green, two white shirts to wear under the sweaters, thick breeches, and a Land Army hat that I never wore once. There were also a green beret, thick socks, immensely heavy shoes, and a pair of rubber boots.

"Warm, but hardly smart," Hilary said, as we carried our new things upstairs . . . the *back* stairs. We finished unpacking our possessions and put them away in the big wall cupboard. Hilary had some very attractive wool dresses, and I was glad that I had brought the new dress Mother had given me at Christmas. But I couldn't hope to compete with Hilary, who added a dashing scarlet ski suit to the rest of her wardrobe. Jane's things were very modest.

We were summoned by a bell. "This *is* a boarding school, after all!" said Hilary. And we all gathered in the lecture hall, to be addressed by the lady warden. I never saw her smile all the time I was at Westringham.

She gave us a lecture on what was expected of us and read out the rules, which included "no alcohol allowed in the college, no smoking upstairs, and no firearms." Jane gave a nervous giggle at the last one, and Hilary, huddled into her fur coat, was making notes. "What shall I do with my cannon?" she whispered to me. I giggled, too, and received a look of extreme disapproval from the platform.

"You will go to bed promptly at nine o'clock, and all lights must be out by nine-thirty. Tomorrow morning breakfast will be at eight o'clock; then you will spend the day touring the place. The next day you will start normal working, and rising time will be at five-thirty for everyone. A list will be put on the notice board telling you which group you are in and where you will be working. Normally you will keep the same rota for one week. Groups will study machine-milking, hand-milking, mucking out, poultry work, what agriculture is possible during winter weather, and so on. One or two girls have requested to work at horticulture. There is little demand for this, but the girls in question have already been promised jobs. I hope all this is quite clear? Then dismiss."

By then it was eight-thirty. We returned to our huddle around the fire. Hilary, still in her fur coat, prowled about on the outside of the group. "I don't know about you girls, but I absolutely refuse to go to bed without a hot water bottle. Being farsighted, I brought one. All I need is a kettle."

"You'll never find one," said one of the Blondes. I knew she was the London one, because she had just been talking about her job in the reception office of a big hotel and bemoaning the fact that she had ever given it up. "Just because I was such a great coward and thought I'd be safer in the country."

"Oh, will I not?" asked Hilary, and marched out of the room. Within ten minutes she was back, clasping in her arms a bulging rubber hot water bottle. We all shrieked, the London Blonde coughed pathetically, and Hilary gave a sardonic smile.

"I penetrated to the kitchen regions and there, lo and behold, was a kettle just on the boil. But I met the Potter woman as I was coming out and she informed me that we are not allowed *near* the kitchens. However, for this one night I shan't freeze."

"We'd better buy a kettle," I suggested brilliantly. "And boil it in here on our fire."

"Twenty-five times," said Misty sadly.

A girl with an ugly, humorous face, who had told us that her name was Marilyn Jameson and she had been a typist in a Manchester office, said, "I used to have an aunt lived near Westringham. It's only a small place, but there are a few shops. One of us could buy a good big kettle on Saturday afternoon. And anyone who hasn't brought a hot water bottle could buy one, or write home for one."

Promptly at nine o'clock Miss Potter appeared and ordered us up to bed. Our room seemed more icy than ever and Jane and I shivered wretchedly as we ventured to the bathroom. Hilary had the minimum wash and was soon in bed, where she lay hugging her hot water bottle and staring at us. I found it embarrassing to undress in front of her, because my underclothes were rather childish, and I dived as quickly as I could into my pajamas. Even those were youthful when compared with hers, which were dark red, piped with black.

I felt so terribly homesick that I thought I would never bear it, yet I had to, for I couldn't be beaten by rules, cold, and twenty-five strange women.

Hilary reached for a notebook and began to make pencil notes. I had a horrible feeling that she was making notes about me and wished I could retaliate by making a drawing of her. A journalist . . . she was probably going to write funny articles about her experiences.

Jane and I got into our ice-cold beds and lay shivering. Suddenly the door opened and Miss Potter stood there. She was probably about Hilary's age and was rather like one of the teachers at my school. Brisk, unattractive, and with darting eyes that missed nothing.

"It's one minute *after* nine-thirty, and your light isn't out."

Hilary slowly closed her notebook. "We err, I see, but it's my fault. Is it really necessary to have so many irksome rules?"

"Yes," said Miss Potter, and snapped out the light. "It is, Miss Buckden. You didn't see the last lot. Well, the first lot. They were a very mixed bag and some had to be watched. Good night. I hope you sleep well."

"Dear me!" said Hilary. "And I imagine this lot is a mixed bag, too. Do you plan any orgies, children?"

I was beginning to find her strange way of talking very amusing indeed, but I hardly knew how to counter it.

"I know I'll never sleep a wink," said Jane, and her voice sounded wobbly.

"You'd better. There's a hard day ahead, with a great many new and possibly unpleasant experiences. But cheer up! The place may look enchanting in daylight, and Mr. Blane may have the heart of an angel."

"I don't like him," I said.

"Ah, poor boy! He has a hard task if he's going to instruct twenty-five inexperienced females, some of them with galloping consumption. I suspect he comes from my native county."

"Shropshire?" I asked. "But you don't talk like that."

"I went to school in the South and have lived away from home for many years. But I know that accent.

Softer than Welsh, yet close to it. Maybe he's a woman hater. I can't wait to see how he reacts to our Misty, and to those Blondes."

I laughed and felt better. How Mr. Blane would react to me was too alarming a thought to contemplate.

One thing about Land Army uniform, it was gorgeously warm. And we needed every layer of clothing we could manage as we assembled outdoors just before nine o'clock the next morning. It was a raw, bitterly cold day, with mist lying over the fields. The great Victorian house loomed over us, with turrets and ornate gables, and beyond a wide lawn there was a lake. It had been the home of a great industrialist before it was turned into a college.

"I never saw a sicker lot!" Hilary murmured in my ear. "You, Primrose, are one of the few with a good color and no hacking cough. Think you'll survive?"

"I just have to," I said. Actually I felt better that morning, and quite eager for all the new experiences. But I was worried about Jane, who said she had hardly slept.

We spent the whole day touring the place. We went from the orchards and gardens and greenhouses to the poultry farm and piggeries. My head was soon crammed with information—two ways of growing blackberries . . . English lights . . . Dutch lights . . . lettuces . . . semi-intensive method . . . Battery B . . .

Khaki Campbells . . . incubators. I hated seeing the battery hens and was glad they weren't all kept prisoner like that. Hundreds of hens and ducks were free, and tiny chickens were warmed by lamps.

It grew colder, and the lectures at each place were long. We had been divided into two parties, and Mr. Blane had the other one. Our instructor was a Mr. Owen, a Welshman, who was gentle and unalarming. After midday dinner we went to the two farms and inspected cows and horses, as well as the dairy, where the real dairy students, who lived in a house across the park, were learning cheese and butter making. They were the last of the peacetime students at the college.

At the Home Farm the cows were Shorthorns, and at the South Farm Ayrshires. The Ayrshires had very engaging expressions and were beautifully marked, but we were told they were jumpy and had to be treated carefully. At the Home Farm we inspected an Alfa Laval milking machine, and at the South Farm the mysteries of an auto-recorder were explained. The Blondes, who were with us, coughed and sneezed most of the time, and Jane wilted and said she had never realized cows were so *large*. Hilary made various *sotto-voce* remarks and looked bored.

By the time we came to farm machinery I think we were all past taking in any more information. Or all but Misty, who had remained bright and interested throughout that long day. What was more, she seemed to have some knowledge. Again and again the blue eyes were raised to Mr. Owen's face—he was quite a tall man—and some intelligent remark made.

"If she's going to flirt with all the men I can see none of us will have a chance," Hilary whispered sourly.

"But she isn't flirting, is she?" I replied. "She's really interested."

"Well, *my* interest is now nil. I could do with a stiff whisky and soda. I suppose the nearest pub is in Westringham, and what hope have we of getting there before Saturday?"

"One of the Blondes has hidden some gin under her mattress," Jane murmured unexpectedly as we moved on.

"Which one?" Hilary asked, with reviving interest. "Bright girl to think of that."

"The one from Bristol, I think. I can only tell them by their voices."

No alcohol in the college. It wasn't likely to trouble me. I felt young, and horribly cold, and my mind had ceased to function.

Finally, as darkness fell, the two parties met in an unheated room in the park and were addressed by the principal of the college. He was a big man, and he seemed not to be very enamored with the horde of future Land Girls. We must learn all we could in the few weeks we had at Westringham. It would be a hard life, and would grow harder, but he assumed we knew that.

Most of us would be employed on small farms, and our pay would be poor. Just twenty-eight shillings and eight pence a week, and half of that would be kept by the farmer for our board. Overtime, if we were lucky. "But then," he said, unsmiling, "male farm workers only get a basic wage of thirty shillings a week, and usually a tied—free—cottage and free vegetables and milk. Tonight there will be a lecture at the house, and tomorrow you will start work. The lists will be up on the notice board when you get back. Good luck."

The lists *were* up. Hilary, Jane, and I were to work together. Hilary said, "Well, little ones, up and at 'em!" We were down for machine-milking and general farming, report at the Home Farm shippons at six o'clock the next morning. A second group, Misty, Marilyn, and the London Blonde, were also on the same rota.

We reported. It was black dark as we went across the park, and there had been a hard frost. The shippons, as cowsheds were called in Cheshire, were dimly lighted and blessedly warm, but there was a strong smell of cow. Jane murmured that she wouldn't dare to go near the great beasts, but she had no choice. Mr. Blane came up to us briskly. He wore a dazzlingly white coat and sounded as irritable as he had done on the first day.

"Put on these black mackintosh aprons, and here are buckets of hot water, scrubbing brushes, currycombs, and cloths. Cleanliness is all important. What's your name? Jane? Start at the top on this side and see that each udder is absolutely *clean*. Primrose? What a name! Start here. And you"—he gave Hilary a long look— "here. Be calm and gentle, but do it thoroughly."

I began to work gingerly along a long row of cows, dabbing each full udder nervously, shrinking back from an impatient hoof. It was winter and the cows were in all day; some of them had lain in the muck. I was called back and shown how to wash each teat with a brisk, firm movement, and how to scrub and comb the hocks.

Halfway along I came near Hilary, who murmured, "Shattering, isn't it? I've never had to deal with a cow's private parts before." I giggled, side-stepped, and my bucket of water went over. Mr. Blane was on me in a second.

"Careless girl! We can't waste time while you frolic and play. Do you think you'll ever make a farm worker?"

I picked up my empty bucket and looked squarely at him. He wasn't so very much taller than myself. Horrible, bad-tempered young man. It had been an accident.

"Yes, Mr. Blane," I said. "I'm going to be one."

"Then get a move on. Wash that cow and fetch a unit. I want to see you put it on."

I obeyed. I would be a farm worker if it killed me, and it seemed very likely to do so.

"In the Bleak Midwinter"

The milking machine was a nightmare of pink rubber tubes and shining metal. I made a complete botch of trying to fit the unit onto the cow's udder and the whole contraption fell to the floor, which, though recently swept, had just collected another dollop of muck.

The more irritated Mr. Blane grew, the more shaky and stupid I felt, and Jane fared little better. We were told to stand and watch, but to keep out of the way of the men. For, though Mr. Blane was instructing us, there were several men doing the bulk of the milking. There were sixty milking cows in two long double shippons, and Misty, Marilyn, and the London Blonde were in the other one.

Hilary got her unit onto the cow, but the animal promptly side-stepped and kicked. "Uncooperative beast!" she muttered venomously, as she joined us as an observer.

It was impressive to watch the efficiency of the men, and the shippon was very quiet, with only an occasional rustle and the steady click of the machinery. Mr. Blane

constantly came up to us and pointed out some proce-
dure, or explained how the milk was drawn until there
was little left in the udder. Then the last drops were
stripped by hand to prevent disease in the udder.

The milk of each cow had to be weighed and the
amount entered on a chart in the milk house, and, when
my turn came, I even made a mess of that and entered
the amount in the wrong column. By then I was feeling
sick, hungry, and tense with nerves.

We met the other three in the milk house, and only
Misty looked cheerful. "Easy," she said. "I've used a
machine before."

"Not so Misty!" I murmured maliciously to Hilary.

Mr. Blane finally dismissed us to breakfast. "You must
remember, girls, that in a few weeks' time you may be
in charge of your own milking herd."

"Heaven forbid!" Hilary said under her breath and
put on her thick raincoat and marched out into the icy
morning. It was just growing light. We other five followed her, in a close group.

"How do you get on with her?" Misty asked, in a low
voice. "There's a rumor she's been an actress, and a
journalist."

"I bet she still is a journalist," I said. "But she isn't
any better than the rest of us, even if she is so old and
experienced in other things. She makes me laugh. I
like her."

After breakfast we were sent to the scullery of the
dairy. This was a place so filled with steam that it was

like a thick November fog all the time. There were four great sinks, two filled with very hot water and two with cold, and a huge sterilizer. It was the steam jet that made the atmosphere so awful. This was for sterilizing the churns, or tankards, as they were called, and it was rather a dangerous business, as the steam was always at boiling point and the tankards grew untouchable in a minute or two. In charge of the dairy was a stern Scotswoman, Mrs. MacDonald, who never stopped talking about invisible dirt.

We spent the morning, and many mornings, scrubbing tankards and milking cans. It was heavy work, as the tankards were fifteen-gallon size and difficult to manipulate in water. We grew very wet and very exhausted, but in a way I found it exhilarating. But Jane grew paler and paler and suddenly had to rush out to be sick.

"Just nerves, poor child," said Hilary. "She'll never make it. Not strong enough."

Mrs. MacDonald took no notice of Jane's white face, and, in fact, the attitude of the whole staff toward illness was very unsympathetic. "You'll find that farmers have little sympathy if you're not feeling well," Mr. Blane said once. "The mangels have to be hoed, or the hay brought in, if you're dying."

Some of the men did show occasional weakness when a few of the girls resorted to what Hilary called flirting, and they would take over some heavy task, like pushing laden barrows. But they never did it for any of us three, and I wouldn't have liked it if they had. I had undertaken to be a farm worker, and I didn't want to use sex appeal to get my work done for me. Not that I seemed to have any appeal for Mr. Blane.

In the afternoon of that first working day we helped to take hay and chopped turnips over the half-frozen fields to some sheep, mucked out several pigsties ("How distressingly loathsome, my children!" said Hilary), and returned to the shippons for evening milking, where we were not much more successful than in the early morning, being by then very cold, tired, and hungry.

"And so ends the first day," said Hilary, as we tramped back to the house through the darkness just in time for supper at six.

But that wasn't the end. We had to assemble in the lecture hall after the meal for study hour, when we were supposed to read agricultural literature and write up our day's notes. The room was bitterly cold, and everyone yawned and coughed and muttered rebelliously.

"Oh, dear God!" groaned Hilary, as we fought for places near the common-room fire later. "Why was I such a fool? Why were you all such fools, girls?"

I was so tired I couldn't keep my eyes open, but in my heart I knew I had enjoyed some of it.

Two weeks passed. We had settled into a kind of routine in the house, though our free time was minimal, and everyone now had a hot water bottle. We had ac-

44

quired a large kettle on the first Saturday, and after study hour we crouched around the fire watching that kettle boil. As each triumphant person filled her hot water bottle she slipped upstairs with it, and there was an element of adventure about this, as one of the rules was that we must not go upstairs without the warden's permission. I thought it was fun, for I was close enough to school discipline not to mind the absurdity of it, but most of the others resented it bitterly.

During those two weeks the weather had settled into the coldest winter for years. Everything froze, and the icy atmosphere of the drafty old house was pretty awful. The pipes were frozen up most days and no water came from the taps, and the sanitation didn't work. The row of bath cubicles in the basement might as well not have been there, for we couldn't use them. Our soap and toothbrushes froze, and the bedrooms were so cold that some people took to going to bed still fully clothed in their sweaters, breeches, and thick socks. Miss Potter discovered this, and after that there was a strict rule we must change into ordinary clothes after supper.

We were a closed community, and I learned more about life in those two weeks than I ever had at school. Some of it secretly shocked me, and occasionally Hilary would raise her eyebrows at Jane and me and say, "Close your ears, little ones. This isn't for such innocent flowers."

"Are we going to stay innocent on farms?" I asked boldly, and she laughed. "I fear not, sweet Primrose.

45

Unless you're turned down as unsuitable, you're going to have to face raw and painful life in the country."

"We can't be turned down," I answered, with fear, for we knew by then that, after a month, we would be assessed.

Several times different instructors had muttered about some girls being too young, and they had meant Jane and me. We were both nervous, and, though we tried desperately hard, we often made absurd mistakes, like the times Jane let out about a hundred hens and forgot to fill the lamps that warmed the baby chicks. My worst sins were continued stupidity over the milking machine (until our group was moved to Young Stock) and giving the wrong amount of feed to the calves. I had always thought calves would be charming creatures, but I hadn't known their awful strength when trying to eat out of a bucket. Not only did I give them the wrong mix, but several times I ended up in the muck with the bucket on top of me. These jaunts into the sheds where the calves were kept took place first thing on such icy mornings that I had no feeling in my hands, anyway. And, after a week or two, the frost gave place to deep snow, which went over the tops of our boots so my feet were wet and frozen, too.

But it was blessed to get away from Mr. Blane, and our new instructor, Mr. Drew, seemed much kinder, but he had tricks up his sleeves. There were several well-grown young bulls, and I was terrified of the white one called Billy. Hilary's story turned out to be true,

because at six-thirty one morning I found myself saun-
tering down the drive with Billy on a short pole. He
pranced and tried to buck, and my empty stomach
heaved with terror. Yet there was a strange fascination
in walking through the snow before it was light, seeing
the branches of the lime trees dimly above me.

Hilary, too, took the bull for a walk. She started with
a certain panache, but the pole came unhooked and
Billy dashed away, to be caught and held by Mr. Drew.
"These beasts are what you might call characters," said
Hilary. "Methinks I'll seek machinery."

And, during the next two days, she was missing from
our group. At supper on the first day she disappeared
she was wearing a smug smile. "Children dear, I pulled
it off. Mr. Blane let me drive one of the lorries. I know
he doesn't exactly warm your heart, Prim, but he's a
nice young man when his temper cools. His people have
a farm near the River Severn a few miles north of
Shrewsbury. His gripe is that he was supposed to be a
college lecturer to genuine students. He got the job
when he was twenty-four, only a few months before
war was declared. Then he found himself faced with
assorted women from all walks of life and not a clue
about the country."

"That's too bad," I said unsympathetically. "Anyway,
he'll probably be called up and that will settle *him*."

"I doubt it. He's in a reserved occupation."

I had never forgiven Mr. Blane for making me feel
silly on so many occasions. I knew I would have done

better if he had not been so sarcastic. And we still weren't free of him, for he supervised certain outdoor jobs during the daytime.

The very sight of his dark good looks, one taste of his overbearing and disapproving manner, and Jane and I were demoralized. He expected us to be fools, and, presto, we did something foolish. It was extremely humiliating, because I really was growing more confident and was learning fast. One wouldn't have thought it a difficult task to feed young pigs, but it was hell. There were hundreds of them, and the moment one appeared with buckets they turned into a screaming mass of pink flesh and open mouths—writhing, shoving, climbing on each other's backs. *And* the first morning we had to feed them there was Mr. Blane in charge, as Mr. Drew had twisted an ankle. We let ourselves in and closed the low gate behind us, and after that . . . chaos. Hilary did manage to tip her two buckets of pig food into the trough, but Jane, besieged on all sides, poured hers over the heads of the nearest, then bolted to the gate. I saw nothing but open mouths and squirming pink flesh before I slipped on some muck and fell flat on my *face*. Small pigs' trotters trampled painfully all over me as the hordes fought for the food that had shot out of my buckets.

I had been cold when I started, and now I hurt all over and the entire front of my raincoat was covered with pig muck. It was even up my nose. I fought my way out, almost crying with pain and humiliation, and that wretched Mr. Blane said, "Well, you really are our funny girl, Primrose Harvey. I asked you to feed the pigs, not to wallow in front of them. Wipe your face and get on with the job, or we'll be here all day."

I had at least had the sense to retrieve my buckets. I was within an ace of swinging one of them and clouting that unsmiling face. Smelling very high, aching and furious, I refilled my buckets and went into the next enclosure. It was a long time before I trusted pigs *or* Mr. Blane.

It snowed and froze and snowed again. The local people were skating on our lake and we watched them with envy. The only one of us who had skates was Misty and she cut a dashing figure on Saturday and Sunday afternoons.

In our third week we were delegated wholly to the poultry farm, which we viewed as light relief, as hens and ducks were a lot less alarming than cows, bulls, and cart horses. The only thing we were afraid of was that we might have to wring some necks, but this was never forced on us. Only the girls who were specializing in poultry had to do it.

Being on the poultry farm turned out to be astonishingly hard work, partly because the snow was so deep and we had to walk miles carrying buckets of hen food or desperately trying to trundle laden barrows to the refuse heaps. Cleaning out hen houses was a revelation to me, because hens made such a lot of muck. And hen dirt smelled far worse than cow muck.

Hilary, relegated to cleaning out the ducks, cursed volubly and staggered to the midden with barrow loads of muck. "Darned dirty devils!" she complained, meeting Jane and me. "I think it's high time I did a little more driving."

The cold was so intense that it was almost frightening. The ducks' water froze almost as soon as we put it out, and one morning our *noses* froze; that did alarm us. But I have several enchanting memories. I shall never forget processions of little khaki ducks coming across the hard snow in a rainbow dawn.

Hilary did go driving, and next day Jane and I worked alone. Hilary went into Crewe to pick up some small machine parts that had been left at the station there, as our local line was blocked by snow.

I didn't mind working alone with Jane, though it was less amusing than when Hilary was with us. But Jane, who had seemed so colorless in the early days, had turned out to be a very good companion. I had admired her from the first because she stuck so grimly to every task, even when she didn't feel very well, and I learned to admire her still more. As we worked she talked, and I soon knew all about her early life, when she was so happy with her parents. Then had come the tragedy of their deaths. Her tales of the orphanage were often funny, and she admitted that everyone had been kind, but it wasn't like family life and she had often been lonely. At eleven years old she had won a scholarship to a high school, but had not been allowed to accept it. The idea was that the young orphans wouldn't need higher education.

"And now I'm free, Prim," Jane said. "Living on a farm may not be a lot better than being in service, but it's for our country, isn't it? And of course we may all die."

"Die?" I asked, startled, for I had forgotten the thoughts I had had when war was declared.

"Well, they say there'll be air raids when spring comes, and the Germans could win, I suppose. We could all starve if they closed all the ports and food got more and more scarce. But if I can help to bring in one harvest . . ."

"We *can't* lose the war," I said, standing with snow over the tops of my boots in the darkening poultry farm.

"One side has to," said Jane.

"But . . . but God must be on our side," I said uncertainly.

"Why should He take sides at all, if He exists?" Jane's voice was calm. "I have no particular reason to believe in God, Prim."

Jane had one talent, and we found out about it a few days after we arrived at the college. Someone said in the common room, "If we had a piano or a gramo-

51

phone we could dance, and that would warm us up."
The Bristol Blonde cried, "Without men? I don't call
that fun."

"We haven't even a radio in this nunnery," Marilyn
grumbled. "Oh, isn't it *boring*, girls!"

Jane slipped away and went illicitly upstairs. When
she came back she held a long, thin whistle in her hand.
She began to pour out a stream of sweet, clear notes
and soon the room was filled with rhythm. Scottish airs,
Irish, and several tunes that I vaguely recognized. We
had done English country dancing at school. All our
feet began to tap, and even Hilary was approving and
called her a clever child.

After that she carried her pipe in her pocket and
would sometimes play us home through the icy darkness. She couldn't read a note of music, but she had an
endless fund of tunes, and now, when I hear some of
the ones she played during those days at Westringham,
I am immediately back there. "In the Bleak Midwinter," Jane piped, as we walked through the snow, and
the modal notes struck me to the heart.

I Discover a New Skill

The days and weeks passed, and I think we had all given ourselves up so wholly to life at Westringham that we had ceased to think that it would end for us. In spite of the awful cold, and the hardships, I adored the time at Westringham. I was often so tired and frozen I wondered if I would be ill, but I never even caught a cold in my head. I was often humiliated by my own stupidity, scared and bewildered by some new task, but I was *living*, as I felt I had never lived at home.

I never wanted to escape from Westringham, as some of the others did. Hilary liked nothing better than to get away, and a few spent what time they could at the nearest pub. Several times the Blondes returned to college slightly the worse for drink, but only we knew. On one occasion the London Blonde arrived back at ten o'clock at night completely drunk (some nameless man had dumped her at the door), and this was treated by the lady warden and the head of the college as a major crime.

I found a great deal that was wildly funny. When I

should have been reading agricultural literature during study hour I often did pencil drawings, and the others soon found out. Especially acclaimed were the one of Hilary clutching her hot water bottle and facing Miss Potter on the Golden Staircase, the one of me flat on my back with a calf staring down at me inquiringly and a bucket upturned on my stomach, and one of Mr. Blane shaking his fist at Hilary while the teat cups of her milking unit lay in the muck under the rear end of a cow. I wrote captions for all of them: "Even if I am serving my country in *its* hour of need, *I* need me hot bottle." "Aren't you going to feed me?" And "I don't know what's going to happen to the milk production of this country."

Another that was admired was a picture of Hilary trying to push a cannon under her bed, with the caption: "Positively no firearms allowed in the college."

I didn't have the time or energy left to write many letters but I sent a few sketches to Mother, along with brief notes.

In our fourth week the threshing machine arrived, and life was a maze of nonstop action, flying chaff, and dust. The chaff got up our noses, into our ears, and stuck agonizingly to our socks. We couldn't even have baths to remove the worst of the itchy dirt, as the baths in the basement were so rarely in action.

One morning the cold was so intense that we were allowed to get up late, and we polished harness until the snow stopped and threshing could start.

Around the middle of that fourth week, as we were walking tiredly back to the house, covered in dust and choking with thirst, Hilary said to me, "Prim, may I borrow some of those drawings of yours? I want to show them to someone. I think he'll be amused." And, all unsuspecting, I gave them to her.

On the Friday I was vaguely aware that I had displeased some of the instructors, and the lady warden seemed to regard me with a very cold eye at midday dinner. "What have I done?" I asked Jane, and she answered, "I don't know, but Hilary's done it, too."

"Hilary?"

"Yes, the warden's just asked her into her office."

"It can't be the same thing," I said, and we went back to the threshing machine without Hilary, who was, in any case, driving a lorry that day. I never even thought of those drawings, and we returned exhausted to find our mail awaiting us in the hall. There was a newspaper for Marilyn, and she unwrapped it, looking puzzled. We never saw newspapers at Westringham, unless someone sent a copy to one of the students.

"Prim!" Marilyn cried, as I was just about to carry Charlie's letter up the back stairs. Hilary had a paper, too, I noticed, but she had tucked it unopened under her arm. She had arrived alone from the opposite direction.

"What?" I asked, and Marilyn held the opened *Manchester Evening News* of the previous day under my nose. My own drawings sprang out at me. SO YOU WANT

TO JOIN THE LAND ARMY? headed the article in huge letters, then the words: "By Hilary Buckden, with drawings by Primrose Harvey."

A strong arm came around my shoulders, and Hilary's deep, drawling voice said, "O.K. You can read my copy. Come on up."

Dazed, I obeyed, and we reached our room, Hilary said, "I meant to tell you tonight, Prim. You'll get at least a pound for each of those pictures. I know I should have asked you, but I wasn't even sure they'd publish the article, let alone shove it in at once. Read it."

I read it, laughing aloud. It was devastatingly funny, giving what was actually a perfectly true picture of our life at the college. But, since they all seemed to lack a sense of humor, no doubt the warden, Mr. Blane, and the rest had not been pleased to be lampooned.

Jane read it, too, and laughed until she cried. "But they won't like you. You'll be in trouble," she said.

"I *am* in trouble," Hilary answered lightly. "But I have my living to earn. They all read the paper last night. But I do assure you, Prim, I told the warden you did it all unwittingly."

"I didn't do those drawings unwittingly," I said. I was scared, excited, and flattered. I had dreamed of being some kind of artist, but it had been a dream of the far future.

"Don't worry. You'll hear no more about it," Hilary said. "But you could easily sell others, you know. Why not send a few to *Cheshire Life?*"

The next day, Saturday, it was borne in on me that sometime that fascinating, uncomfortable life would end, for several of the girls heard from their regional secretaries that jobs had been found for them. The Bristol Blonde was to go to a farm in Somerset at the end of the following week, and a little pretty thing called Joyce Benn, who came from Suffolk, was to go to a poultry farm there and rear incubator chicks. As these bits of news were imparted, Hilary grew despondent and said, "Oh, how tired I am of these stupid regulations! Children dear, I yearn for London, but I'd even be glad to get away to a farm. We could hardly be worked harder than we are in this darned place."

Jane and I looked at each other. Hilary had gradually managed to do rather less work than anyone; she didn't exactly flirt with the instructors, but she had a clever trick of engaging them in conversation.

That afternoon we joined the skaters on the frozen lake, though only to slide like children in a quiet corner. Misty skimmed about among the local people, and we eyed her enviously. Then Hilary appeared, wearing her scarlet ski suit, with a pair of skates dangling from her hand.

"I borrowed them from Mr. Blane," she said laconically.

"Mean to say he's forgiven you for the article?" I asked, for he didn't seem to have forgiven me. That morning he had been in charge of a party taking great loads of turnips over the snowy fields to the sheep, and it had spoiled my pleasure to see his eyes on me. I *loved* journeys through the snow, but I couldn't enjoy myself with that wretched man looking disapproving. All the same, the memory of my success had kept me awake for an hour the previous night. If the war ever ended, if we *won*, as we had to do, I would get somewhere . . . I would!

Oh, it was enchanting on the frozen lake. The great house loomed darkly against a sky laden with snow, and the ice was covered with gaily dressed skaters. At dusk, laughing and happy, we returned to the house, and there, on the board in the hall, was a new notice that said: "Will the following students attend outside the warden's office at five-thirty: Primrose Harvey, Jane Preston, Hilary Buckden, Claudia Ray."

Consternation on the part of Jane and myself, and all happiness fled. Hilary was airy and bored, and Claudia Ray, the London Blonde, said, "What the dickens have I done now?"

We washed as best as we could, as there was no hot water, and, shivering violently, put on our clothes for the evening. Then we waited in the alcove off the hall, outside the lady warden's door. Jane was called in first, and she was there maybe five minutes. She came out white as a sheet, her brown eyes wide and filled with tears.

"She says . . . she says I'm not suitable for the Land Army. I'm too young and not the right type. They need stronger girls on farms. And I've done *everything*! No one ever helped *me* to push a barrow."

I felt sick. I was scared at the prospect of going to a lonely farm, but by then I was deeply held in the queer fascination of hard work against odds, even though some of the work was so awful, like feeding those wretched pigs. I wanted to be in the country when spring and summer came, and, besides, I couldn't face Mother, Charlie, and my friends if I were turned down.

"Have you to leave then, little one?" Hilary asked.

"No-o. She said, quite n-nicely, that she was just advising me, and she would consult the regional office. I'm to stay until she hears from them, and . . . and go on to hand-milking tomorrow."

Hand-milking! I hated the machines, but by then I longed to try to hand-milk. I stumbled into the office, shivering with cold and nerves.

The warden said much the same to me as she had said to Jane. I was very young and not perhaps a tough enough type to live on a farm. "Besides," she said, fixing me with a not unkindly gaze, "we feel that your attitude may be a little too frivolous, Primrose."

Those drawings! But why shouldn't it all be funny? I choked, gasped, and said, "But I do love it. There's an awful lot to learn, and we've all done silly things, but . . ."

"Stay until you hear from the regional secretary," she said. "But do consider what I say. There must be something else you would like to do."

But there was nothing. I couldn't even imagine the outside world of war, and towns, and people I used to know. More than four weeks at Westringham had conditioned me to the rhythm of the country in wintertime.

Jane was still there when I came out, and we stood huddled together. Jane sobbed quietly, saying she wouldn't go back to the orphanage and be found another job in service. I didn't cry, but my throat was tight and my eyes burned. The London Blonde said, "Cheer up, you kids! It's an awful life, anyway. If I'm chucked out I'm going back to London tomorrow, and if I'm killed in an air raid at least it'll be in a place that I know."

Hilary came out looking cool and sardonic. "I am hardly the type. Too sophisticated, and I don't take the work seriously. But I am to join you two little ones at hand-milking tomorrow morning, pending communication with my regional secretary."

We didn't wait for the Blonde. Hilary said, "Now cheer up, children. You will probably find yourselves on farms. I've heard there's some lack of communication between the college and the regional offices, which are mostly run by well-meaning but not very efficient women. Meanwhile, I shall think seriously. Do I *want* to be a farm worker? Right now we're quite well fed and have a roof over our heads."

When we got up at five-thirty on Sunday morning it was snowing hard and a high wind was howling. We hurried, shivering, into our clothes and hastily drank

the hot tea that was always ready before we went outdoors. During a sleepless two hours I had determined
to enjoy every second of Westringham while I had it
and try not to worry about the future. The only thing
that bothered me was that I would be under Mr. Blane
again. I was ten times more confident than I had been
in the beginning, but something about that young man
still ruffled me, and I knew I would do better with
someone else.

We fought our way through the blizzard to the regi-
mented peace of the great shippon. The men were
moving quietly about giving the cows their feed, and
the air was warm. Mackintosh aprons awaited us, and
cloths, buckets, milking cans, and stools. The cows to
be hand-milked were standing at the end of the shippon, eight of them. By then we had had many lectures
on milk production, milk yields, and the diseases to
which milking cows were prone, so we already knew
that we had to take a test squirt from each teat into a
special cup.

My stomach settled when I saw that Mr. Blane was
not there. We were in the charge of the nice Mr. Graham we had met during other tasks. He had an easy,
pleasant manner, so I washed my allotted cows with a
panache that rivaled Hilary's and accomplished the job
without disaster.

Mr. Graham sat down on a stool, put his left knee
against the cow's flank, and the pail in place. He then
showed me how to hold the teat, and the gentle but

firm movement that would draw the milk. Then he handed can and stool to me.

The cow was munching peacefully, the atmosphere was calm and relaxing. I sat down and put my hands on two of the teats. They were warm, yielding and soft, rather nice, in a way, yet for a moment I felt a wild panic. Then a miracle happened. Suddenly I knew exactly how to do it. And did it. My hands and fingers moved and milk flowed with a delicious purring sound into the pail. The cow continued to eat, just as if there wasn't a stranger performing such an intimate task. The milk frothed and mounted in the pail, and I was hypnotized by my own rhythm.

It was splendid; a real achievement. I leaned my forehead against the beast's warm side and sat on, changing to the two other teats when it seemed that the milk was almost finished. Jane, Hilary, and Mr. Graham stood there watching me, in silence.

"Very well done!" Mr. Graham said at last. "I can see you're a natural. Now this is how you strip the last drops." And he took my place and showed me the delicate movement.

I weighed the milk and entered it on the chart, filled with triumph and a strange joy. When I returned to the shippon Jane wasn't doing badly, but Hilary, with puckered brow and muttered curses, was struggling unavailingly with her cow.

"The confounded beast doesn't like me," she said to

me, when Mr. Graham moved away. "I can't imagine how you did it, child."

"Neither can I," I agreed, but I repeated the performance with my next cow, though she wasn't giving so much milk.

They couldn't throw me out when I was a natural milker; they couldn't! I struggled back to the house through the slow and icy dawn, happier, perhaps, than I had ever been in my life, just because of my contact with a large dumb beast.

A Baby and a Lamb

After breakfast the London Blonde departed to catch a train to Crewe, where she would change to an express. Our local line was open again.

When Jane and I were making our beds, Hilary brought up the news that Mr. Blane had left the previous evening to go home to Shropshire. His father was desperately ill, believed to be dying. I knew I ought to be sorry but I was flooded with relief, because now I could enjoy each session of hand-milking to the full.

Oh, how quickly that week at Westringham passed. Milking seemed to follow close on milking, yet we did a great many other things. We spent three days on horticulture, which was boring, and I resented the time spent away from "real farming." We washed endless plant pots and did various tasks in the greenhouses. It was warm and peaceful, but I would so much sooner have been fighting through the snow to take food to the outlying animals.

It was a relief to be back on general farming. At least

Jane and I felt it was; Hilary said she liked being a turnip in a warm greenhouse.

Nothing more was said about leaving, so presumably no communication had come about us. But most of the other students had now heard they had been found jobs. By the next Saturday everyone had departed and a new lot had moved in. Hilary had somehow acquired a tiny room to herself, and Jane and I found ourselves sharing with one of the newcomers, a very shy girl who had worked in a factory. It was wonderful to be "old girls."

We had been left on hand-milking, to my deep, secret joy. Hilary was much less joyful. Her struggles with a cow she called Three-teat Thelma were very funny, and I did a drawing with the caption: "I'll get some milk out of you if it kills both of us!"

On the Monday morning, Mr. Blane was back. I washed my cows and settled down to milk, and at first he took no notice of me. One of the men seemed to have a problem and he went away to talk to him. By the time he came back I was just finishing my first cow. He loomed over me, saying in a bored voice, "Are you having trouble? Let me see what I can do."

I rose without a word and handed him my almost full can. Finding it so unexpectedly heavy, he nearly dropped it. It was a sweet moment. "Oh, you seem to have got quite a lot!" he cried.

I drew myself up to my full height and our eyes met in a curiously aware glance. Even in my moment of triumph and success I saw that he was pale and looked as if he hadn't been sleeping.

"I'm a very good hand-milker," I said, and added, "Mr. Blane," with some emphasis.

"Yes, I see you are, Primrose," he answered, and moved on to Hilary, who was having her usual vicious struggle with Thelma.

"Peter Blane's father is still very ill and he may have to go home again at any time," Hilary told me later that morning.

"Oh, it's Peter now, is it?" I asked.

"Well, dear girl, he is about ten years younger than I am," she said dryly. "He'll have to run the family farm if his father dies. Why do you dislike the poor lad so much?"

"Oh, because . . ." I was not quite sure why I did dislike Mr. Blane. "He made the first days pretty difficult; worse than they would have been otherwise. He's unsympathetic, and self-opinionated, and a woman hater."

"He may be the last," she agreed, lifting a dollop of muck onto her barrow. "He was jilted by a girl at home. She joined the WAAF and said she wasn't going to marry anyone until the war ended."

"Well, I can see why she didn't want to marry him," I said.

That week passed in delicious peace, and it seemed that our regional secretaries had forgotten us. We three were the elite, and it was fun to learn about the new students and watch their struggles. Increasingly our time during the daylight hours was spent carrying food and water to distant animals, for the severe weather showed no sign of abating.

On Friday morning the sun shone brilliantly after breakfast and the sky was blue. The great snowy world gleamed and drew me. When we came downstairs after making our beds the post had come and there was a letter for me from the regional office. All joy fled and fear took its place.

Dear Miss Harvey,

You have now spent several weeks at Westringham College, and I have arranged for you to finish your training at Littlewood Farm, Rillsden, Cheshire. Mr. Farndon will not employ you permanently, as he informs us that he has applied for two boys from a Manchester orphanage. But, meanwhile, he will expect you on Friday, February 16, and will meet you . . .

I stared blankly at the letter. There were also various forms and papers, including a travel voucher. Friday, February 16!

"I've got to go . . . today!" I shouted. "To a farm, to finish my training. Oh, I can't!"

The only people in the hall were Hilary and Jane. Hilary was standing by the door, waiting for us, and Jane was reading a letter. Jane, I noticed, was very pale.

She had looked quite different lately; pink cheeked and in every way more healthy.

"I've got to go to a farm, too," she said. "Today."

"Oh, dear God!" Hilary grumbled. "Am I to be left in this perfectly awful place without you two young ones?"

"To Littlewood Farm, Rillsden," I said. "Where's Rillsden?"

"It's almost a district of Manchester, I think," said Hilary.

"But I'm to go there, too," said Jane.

"Both of us?" I gasped, in relief.

There really couldn't have been any proper communication between the college and the regional secretary. The college said we were unsuitable, and the office said we were to finish our training. The good side of the news began to seep through to me. But, oh, Westringham! The park and fields blazing dead white in the sun, under a blue sky. The shippon waiting for me in the evening.

The warden came out of her office and saw us standing there.

"Miss Preston and Miss Harvey, I am informed that you are to go to Rillsden. Miss Potter will drive you to the station at twelve o'clock. Please be ready."

Hilary, ignoring the day's work, helped us to pack. We had acquired so many things that our suitcases wouldn't hold everything. She found brown paper and string and made the remainder into untidy parcels.

"And you'd better wear your rubber boots. Do for

heaven's sake try to get some of the muck off! I'll tie your shoes to your suitcases."

Jane and I wandered out into the snow and we said goodbye to everyone. Most of the men were very nice and wished us luck. I was glad not to see Mr. Blane around anywhere. I stood for several minutes in the quiet shippon; work there had started as impossibly difficult and had ended as a strange delight. Never again would I sit quietly milking in that ordered atmosphere, never again would I struggle over the fields to the sheep or feed the khaki ducks in a rainbow dawn.

I met Mr. Blane in the doorway as I was leaving. He said, "Oh, Primrose! So you're off?"

"Both of us, Jane and me," I said pointedly. "To finish our training. The Land Army can't get rid of us that easily."

"Evidently not," he said, smiling slightly. "You've turned out better than I thought. I'll advise the office to find you a permanent job on a farm where you can hand-milk. Not that they'll take any notice."

"As they didn't the first time," I said. "You said we were unsuitable."

"Look, I wasn't the only one. The pair of you pulled up. Best of luck wherever you go."

"Thanks," I said, and went into the other shippon to look for Jane. That was the end of Peter Blane. He was going to be the one unpleasant memory of Westringham. Even the horrors of the calves and pigs were already fading into the realms of necessary experience.

We traveled to Crewe, where we had some lunch in

the refreshment room. There were no porters, and our heavy suitcases, dangling shoes, and unsafe parcels were a dreadful burden.

Mr. Farndon was not at the station to meet us. We waited a long time and then took a taxi. Hilary had given me the money for the drawings and I felt rich. We drove out into a flat, snow-laden countryside that didn't look very attractive.

The taxi turned into a lane where the banks were high with packed snow, and then into a farmyard. The farmhouse was on one side, and shippons, barns, pig-sties on the other. A threshing machine was working, and, just as we stepped out of the taxi, the moving belt went still. A red-haired lad on a stack stared at us.

"The back door, I think, girls," said the taxi driver, who clearly knew more about farms than we did. He dumped our possessions on the step and knocked. The door was opened by an untidy, youngish woman, with a small girl at her side. Behind them a baby was screaming.

"Oh, you're the Land Girls!" she said. "My husband went to meet you, but he was late. You must have passed him." We were soon to learn that Mr. Farndon was always late.

The kitchen looked awful, incredibly squalid. It was a terrible shock. Until then, I suppose, I had had an imaginary picture of a farmhouse kitchen as a lovely place, with old scrubbed tables and strings of onions drying and great smoked hams.

The kitchen at Littlewood Farm was nothing like that. Dirty dishes were piled up by the sink, the stone floor was literally filthy, and there was a strong smell of very unclean baby. Mrs. Farndon was quite pretty, but her hair was tangled and her apron horribly stained. The baby continued to scream from a cot in a corner.

"Everything gets me down," she said, as she led us up a narrow staircase. "I've never been right since the boy came. I hope you girls are good workers? John said . . . well, he wants boys to help on the farm, but he thought it might be an idea to train a few girls from the college. They'd help me as well."

To my astonishment Jane said firmly, "We're Land Girls, Mrs. Farndon. We work outdoors, not indoors."

The woman seemed taken aback. "Yes, well. . . . This is your room. Hope you don't mind sharing a bed? You can unpack later. You'd better go out at once. We eat after milking."

She went away and Jane and I surveyed the cold and awful room. There were dingy curtains, linoleum on the floor, and a picture of Queen Victoria over the bed. The bed itself . . . I pulled back the coverlet and whispered in horror, "I don't think the sheets are clean!"

"Nor the towels," Jane agreed, looking at the two gray towels hanging over the bedrail.

"And the paper in the drawers is ages old, and do you think that's mouse dirt?" I asked. I was shivering and felt terrible. We had been warned often that farms might be difficult; that we might be abused or ignored.

71

We had not been told that we might have to sleep in dirty beds.

"I'm going to tackle her," said Jane, and started for the door.

"You'd never dare!"

"Yes, I dare. We have our rights."

Jane went resolutely down the rather dirty stairs, and I followed. My first impression of her as a sick elf had long since faded. The baby was still screaming, and its yells were rivaled by a radio belting out the music of a dance band. The little girl, whose name turned out to be Dolores, was wetting herself quietly in a corner.

Mrs. Farndon listened to Jane's shouted request for clean sheets. "They aren't dirty. Mother was only here for two weeks. Oh, well, if you're so fussy, take some out of the top drawer on the landing. But hurry. John's back."

We changed the sheets, put on our outdoor clothes again, and ventured into the farmyard. Now that it was the middle of February the days were lengthening, but the snow was beginning to turn pink and gold with sunset light. At Westringham milking would be almost over.

A tall man in old farming clothes came across the yard to meet us. At his heels were a black-and-white collie dog and a very small lamb. The lamb was skittering on the frozen, dirty snow and gave an indignant *Baa-a-a!* when its tiny feet slipped. The man, Mr. Farndon, picked the lamb up and said, "This is Sammy. He's

72

on the bottle and has grown very tame. Sorry I missed you girls at the station. Go and help Norman to put the horse in the cart." He waved his hand toward what seemed to be the stables. "There are two dead sheep up the fields that'll have to go on the midden. No hope of burying them while the frost lasts."

"What time do we milk?" I asked, and he laughed. He had a nice face, but he was pale and one eye twitched nervously.

"Time? When all the other work is done, feeding and that. I'll get on feeding the pigs while you just fetch those sheep. Norman! Norman! Here're the girls! You haven't time to be shy."

Norman was the red-haired lad, with a very attractive smile. He looked about sixteen but turned out to be twenty. At school we had learned the English folk song "A Farmer's Son So Sweet," but he was not a farmer's son. He had come from a Manchester orphanage five years before.

We had learned at Westringham how to harness a horse and put him into a cart, so we didn't make fools of ourselves. Norman looked at us in surprise. "Town lasses! Didn't think you'd know anything."

We all climbed up into the cart and jolted over the snowy, frozen fields. We found the sheep, very dead and frozen hard, and put them into the cart. We must have grown fairly tough, because we didn't even shudder. When we returned there were the hens and ducks to feed and lock up, and it was growing dark when we entered the shippon. By then I was dead tired and faint from hunger, and the shock almost made me sick. The place looked as if it hadn't been mucked out for days; buckets and milking units stood in deep filth.

"I can't bear it!" I said to Jane. There was a mixed herd of Shorthorns, British Friesians, and a few Ayrshires, and we had learned enough to see at a glance that they were in fairly bad shape.

Mr. Farndon was close on our heels. "Can you manage the machine, girls? There's no need to do much washing. The inspectors were around last week and won't be back for a while. Besides, the word's always sent ahead, and we're never taken by surprise. Farmers look after each other, like."

All those lessons about *invisible* dirt! Too shocked to answer, I heard Jane saying composedly, "Yes, we used the same machine at college. I think I can manage it. Primrose is a wonderful hand-milker."

"Then she can milk those cows down at the far end."

I milked, but there was no pleasure in it. The cows were giving a poor yield, and two or three were almost dry. One had a bad case of mastitis. The stench got on my empty stomach and I felt so miserable I wondered how I was going to survive Littlewood Farm.

Afterward we all went in for the evening meal. Norman lived at the farm. He was shy and thoroughly nice, but he couldn't possibly understand our feelings; he took it all for granted. Greasy chipped potatoes, the smell of

74

the unchanged baby, the dirty tablecloth. It was awful
. . . awful.

We were expected to eat our pudding off our meat
plates without washing them. Jane and I rose and
washed ours at the sink, and were promptly dubbed
finnicky. Even gentle Norman jeered. "You lasses'll learn
differently when you've been on farms for a bit."

The kitchen, at least, was very warm, with a roaring
fire. The collie lay stretched out in front of it; and the
lamb, Sammy, was there, too. He'd tucked himself
comfortably against the dog's flank.

"We had three lambs indoors, but the other two
died," Mrs. Farndon said. "John lost most of his flock
in the bad weather. It's a darned nuisance, because it
needs a bottle of milk just about as often as the baby.
If you wake up in the night you can come down and
give it one. We try and keep the fire in."

The lamb was enchanting, though I was surprised at
how hard its fleece was.

"Yes, I will," I said, for all of a sudden its life seemed
important. If I could help to save one creature in that
iciest winter for years I would have done something.
But I was horrified by the dirty state of the bottle she
produced and vowed to myself it was going to get a
good sterilizing as soon as possible. Norman showed
me how to hold the bottle, and the lamb, wide awake
in a second at the sight of food, had astonishing
strength. His whole little rear end waggled violently
as he sucked.

Oh, it was down to basics all right. The baby was changed and the dirty nappy left on the table, while he, too, had his bottle. Not much cleaner than the lamb's.

A baby and a lamb. So you want to join the Land Army? I held the bottle with both hands while the lamb fiercely dragged out the last drops.

Too Late to Turn Back

Dolores was given a cursory wash in front of the fire and put into a grubby nightgown. She had a sore mouth and a slight squint, and was not at all an appealing child. I had had a picture of country children as rosy-cheeked, healthy little mortals; *apple*-cheeked, they were sometimes called in books. Dolores looked no better than the slum children of Liverpool.

The dog snored and the radio blared out the war news. The war still seemed very distant. At the far end of the table Mr. Farndon was working at his accounts, his brow puckered. Mrs. Farndon washed some of the dishes and looked reproachfully at us. Jane ignored the looks, but, less strong minded, I took up a dirty towel and wiped a few plates.

Then I went upstairs to get my drawing pad and pencils, and Jane came, too, for her writing materials. We stood in the awful chill of our room and eyed each other.

"Don't they inspect these places?" I asked bitterly.

"They're supposed to," Jane said. "I'm sure we shouldn't have been sent to this kind of farm."

"Well, what can we do? Complain? If we do it may all come out about the college saying we were unsuitable. And it's probably not for long. Our training was supposed to last two months."

"I can put up with it if you can," said Jane.

I nodded, and picked up my writing paper as well as my drawing pad. I had better write and tell Mother where I was.

On the way back to the kitchen we peeped into an icy, unlovely little dining room and a sitting room that looked as if it was never used. It was freezing hard outside and warmth was of paramount importance.

I wrote a short letter to Mother, not giving any description of the place, then sat drawing the dog and the lamb. Mrs. Farndon, who had taken up some dingy knitting, evidently had long sight. She said, in a grudging voice, "That's clever, Primrose. A lovely picture of our Jack and Sammy."

I tore off the sheet and put it up on the mantelpiece, and Mr. Farndon and Norman added their praise. They little knew that I was aching to draw Dolores, and Norman shouldering a dead sheep in the snowbound fields. I *would* do them later. The first I would call "Country Child" and the second "Dead as Mutton."

Finally we went up to bed with the knowledge that at least the sheets were clean, though we had our doubts about the mattress. If Jane hadn't been there with me,

I think I would have died of loneliness and despair. We cuddled each other to try and get warm and laughed under the bedclothes, finding that we could see the funny side of it.

I awoke at three-thirty, put on my slippers and warm coat, and, using my flashlight, slipped quietly down to the kitchen, which was still blessedly warm. The kettle was singing on the hob, and the fire was a banked-up glow. I warmed some milk and filled the bottle, and Sammy was out of his box before it was ready. I sat on the rug and held the bottle out to him, and he tugged and gulped and waggled, nearly pulling the nipple out. It was almost more a dream than anything else had been, feeding a lamb in the middle of an icy February night, at a farm in the flat Cheshire countryside.

Suddenly the strange enchantment possessed me, as it had done on those other occasions—walking the bull down the avenue before dawn, feeding the little khaki ducks in rainbow light. And I *wouldn't* have been home, an ordinary schoolgirl, not for one minute.

Mr. Farndon called us at six o'clock. We had a cup of tea before going outdoors. It was snowing again and it was a relief to get into the warm shippon, though the smell almost made me heave. Jane dealt with the machine, while I firmly washed a few cows before settling down to hand-milking.

Mr. Farndon, seeing we knew what we were about,

went off to the dairy to wash bottles, and after a time Norman came and sat near me, milking the next cow.

"One of you girls'll go on the milk round," he said.

"Milk round?" I asked, startled, and he laughed.

"You must know about milk rounds, even if you are a lady and used to living in luxury."

"I'm not a lady and I didn't. . . . Oh, I mean, yes, I do know about milk rounds," I said, continuing with the gentle rhythm.

"*She* used to wash the bottles and leave the kids in bed. There were two old men, but one's ill and the other retired. Sometimes she went on the round."

"*She?* Mrs. Farndon? Don't you like her?" I asked.

There was a pause; then Norman said, "You watch her, that's all. She'll be jealous of you because you're so young, and pretty, and free. You shouldn't be doing work like this."

"There's a war on," I said, absently using the current catch phrase.

"She's a bad manager," the gentle voice told me. "It gets her down, the cold, and the kids, and everything. She can be spiteful . . . I'm just telling you. But *he's* all right. Works until he drops, though not much of a manager, either. I'll do better if ever I have me own farm. The other girl, Jane, looks delicate, but maybe she'll find it easier, not being a lady. She told me she comes from an orphanage, too."

"Oh, for heaven's sake, stop talking about being a lady!" I said irritably, hoping Jane hadn't heard.

"You're not our kind, but you're a brave lass," said the "Farmer's Son So Sweet." Then he asked suddenly, "Will you come to the cinema with me one night?"

"Why, yes. But Jane must come, too." Probably he wouldn't like that, but I couldn't leave Jane alone in that awful kitchen for a whole evening.

I went on the milk round with Mr. Farndon. Jane stayed to bottle some more milk and start the mucking out. I enjoyed it in a way, though the cold was terrible. It was rather bewildering that first time, but, within a few days, I knew each of the newish houses outside the town, and what milk they required. Some wanted different grades of milk, and this was easily settled by popping different-colored tops on the same bottles. Mr. Farndon seemed to think it rather a joke, and I didn't dare to show how shocked I felt. More and more college ideals dropped into the snow with every hour that passed.

The horse jogged on through the icy morning as the sky brightened and the flakes ceased to fall. I was weak with hunger but, yes, I did enjoy it. The only thing was that I slipped and broke two bottles and sent a cloud of milk spattering up a smart red door. "I ordered two pints, but I prefer not to have it on my new paint," said the lady of the house sourly.

I apologized abjectly to her and Mr. Farndon.

When we got back it was almost nine o'clock but breakfast was not ready. The kitchen stank of baby, hot fat, and an overheated collie and lamb, but when the

food came there was plenty of it and I was too raven-
ous to be fussy.

We spent the day, and most of our days, mucking
out the cows, horses, pigs, and poultry. At least everywhere was soon a lot cleaner than when we arrived.
With the snow lying so deeply there was no hope of
field work, and there were few sheep left. We did odd
jobs, too, like pulping turnips, collecting eggs, and
cleaning harness and machinery. I had an almost con-
stant companion at my heels; a very small but determined lamb.

By Land Army rules we should have had an hour for
dinner and worked only forty-eight hours a week, but
it was impossible to insist on sticking to the rules. I
doubt if many girls managed to do so, on any farm.
Dinner, when we got it, was usually at one-thirty or
later, and Mr. Farndon and Norman went out again
immediately afterward and expected us to follow. We
rarely finished work before seven. In spite of eating
endless chocolate we were always hungry, and it was
agony when meals were late.

Norman proved absolutely right, for Mrs. Farndon
seemed to turn against us, particularly against me. She
resented the fact that we were always outdoors.

On the evening we went to the cinema with Norman
a sow was due to farrow and, when we walked back late
through the falling snow, lights were on and Mr. Farndon was sitting quietly by the sow's heaving side, with
nine piglets already born. The sight moved me deeply,

for it was a totally new experience to see the next piglet slide out into the straw. The dim light, the silence, the snow falling outside made the whole thing seem almost Biblical.

"The lasses shouldn't be here," Norman protested, and Mr. Farndon asked, "Why not? They'll see many animals born if they keep on farming."

When we had been at Rillsden a few days, a parcel came from Hilary containing some things we had left behind and a copy of *Of Human Bondage* for me, a book she had said I ought to read. She had been offered a job in Shropshire driving lorries and tractors, and was leaving the college the next day.

"Will this awful winter never end?" wrote Hilary. "And, even when it does, everyone says the war will be stepped up. Hope you kiddies are surviving. By the way, Peter Blane's father died and he's leaving the college at Easter. They won't release him earlier."

"I wonder if we'll ever see her again?" I asked Jane, as we made our bed. "We know where she is, anyway. She's put her address."

As February passed, the weather improved slightly, but snow still lay in patches on the dreary fields and the new houses near the farm looked raw and unattractive. I longed for prettier country.

We had somehow become used to our life in the cluttered kitchen and had even grown mildly fond of Dolores, and the baby. Sammy grew and prospered, thanks mainly to my regular feeding, and the place was slightly cleaner now that Mrs. Farndon wasn't expected to help in the dairy or with the milk round. But it was a relief to know that our time at Littlewood would end. Mr. Farndon had heard from the orphanage that two boys were coming early in March.

My main pleasures were the lamb and Norman. Norman was a strange young man. He said he liked to be quiet and think, and I knew it really was thinking and not just rustic ruminating.

Norman and Jane got on well together, but I seemed to get an extra sweetness, somehow. I realized, with shock, that he was falling in love with me. He was a very nice person, but love was no good. I would go away, and he wasn't my kind. Yet, when he kissed me in the barn, I couldn't help responding. No one had ever kissed me like that before, ever so shyly and fumblingly.

There came a day in early March when most of the snow had melted and the sun had faint warmth in it. Norman and I worked all day up the fields, uncovering a potato tump. It was heavy work uncovering the tump and tossing the potatoes up into the cart, but there was a certain pleasure in being tired and growing hungry. The afternoon was almost over, and soon we must go to milking.

I stood in the tump, with Norman up in the cart, and suddenly he said, "Prim, have you ever thought? We could get married. I could find a better job, maybe with a nice cottage. As a farm worker I may never be called up. Prim . . ."

I stared up at him blankly and saw his warm, sweet smile. In a kind of way I suppose Norman was simple; very unsophisticated, anyway. Charlie would have laughed at him. He was asking me to *marry* him! Well, I was seventeen; other girls married as young as that. For a wild moment, standing there in the middle of the tump under the pale March sky, I contemplated the possibility. A cottage with Norman, little children with red hair. And then I remembered that a farm worker's wage was thirty shillings a week. Of *course* I couldn't marry Norman. I would need Mother's permission, and she would never give it.

"I shouldn't ask a lady," he said, as I stood in silence. "But . . . but I've grown to love you, Prim, and I'd like to marry, get away from Farndons'."

"Look," I said, "it's not because I'm a 'lady' that I can't marry you." But in a way of course it was. "I do like you, Norman. Maybe I love you in a kind of way. Thank you for asking me, but you'll find someone else."

"No," he said, "I'll join the Army and learn to kill people." And he jumped off the cart and scrambled into the tump. His cold lips met mine, less shyly than before, and we kissed. Oh, yes, he was nice, perhaps the nicest young man I would ever meet, but it was no use.

Sadly I pushed him away and we drove back to the farmyard. If I had saved Sammy (for what? the butcher's knife?) I would probably be instrumental in sending Norman into the Army. I didn't like to picture Norman with no time to "think," marching and maybe fighting in another land. Killing people, my Farmer's Son So Sweet.

The next day Jane and I had letters from the regional office. Mine said: "You have now finished your training for the Women's Land Army. You may go home next Friday for the weekend, then please report at River Farm, Wellshalline, North Shropshire, on Monday, March 11. Mr. Clark will employ you permanently as a milker and general farm worker. Enclosed you will find travel vouchers. It is advised that you travel by train to Shrewsbury and then take a Pritchard's bus, which leaves at two-forty-five from behind the Severn Inn. Mr. Clark will pay you weekly, deducting half your wages for your keep."

"So you're both off?" asked Mrs. Farndon. She sounded pleased, but Dolores began to cry. Mrs. Farndon would be able to bully the two orphanage boys as she sometimes bullied Norman.

"Yes, on Friday," I told her. "Home for the weekend, then to a farm in North Shropshire." And I looked at Jane.

"I'm going to Shropshire, too," she said. "Isn't that funny? Hilary's there, and Mr. Blane will be, after Easter. Melwardine Farm, Melwardine. I have to go to Shrewsbury and then take a bus."

It seemed to be the same bus, which cheered us mightily. It was strange how we had managed to stay together in our new world. "Maybe our farms are quite near," I said hopefully, as we mucked out. "It would be nice if Hilary is near, too, but I certainly never want to see Peter Blane again."

So the last days at Rillsden passed. We hadn't been there many weeks, but it felt like a good part of a lifetime. The snow had gone, Sammy was growing quite big. Norman was quiet and gloomy. Jane said, in the deep privacy of our shared bed, "Norman's upset. He likes you, Prim."

"Yes," I agreed. "I feel . . . well, somehow guilty about him, Jane. He asked me to marry him that day we were on the potato tump."

Jane gave a muffled shriek. "Marry him? You? He must be mad!"

"Mad? He certainly isn't, but I'm afraid I've made him unsettled, and now he'll join the Army and get killed."

"But you couldn't marry him."

"I *know* I couldn't. But, somehow, standing there in the tump, cold and tired, it did seem almost possible. Then I thought of a farm worker's wages, and . . ."

"But you're only a kid," said Jane.

"I'm as old as you." But my voice faltered. She laughed.

"You're not. You may be tall, but there's something wrong. You always look guilty when age is mentioned. That birthday you had at college, when your Mother sent a cake. You said you were eighteen, but I thought . . ."

"You're right. I was seventeen," I confessed. "But don't tell a soul."

"It's no surprise. And Norman's a darling, but he's slightly nutty, too. You'll have to forget him."

But I knew I would never forget Norman, nor cease to feel guilty because I had disturbed his world.

We milked for the last time, and I went on the milk round for the last time. In many ways I wasn't sorry to leave the discomfort and dirt of Littlewood Farm. Our sheets had been clean when we started, but we had never dared to change them, and our towels were black with much use. Home seemed unimaginably far away, but by two o'clock I was back in Wallasey. Mother was at school, but I had spoken to her on the telephone and she had left the key under a pot. It was extraordinary to see my dear room, with my books and pictures. Wonderful to have a hot bath, with delicious warm, clean towels; splendid to cook myself a meal in a clean kitchen. I was so used to my breeches and Land Army sweater that I could hardly bear to leave them off, but they did smell very highly of cows and pigs. When Mother came home and discovered them she shrieked with horror and made me take them to the cleaner's.

Charlie came home from the university and we spent the evening talking. I sank into my dear clean bed, but I did not feel at home. It was utterly wrong not to have to milk, and slave, and be tired and cold.

I told only a carefully edited version of my adventures. They could never understand the hardships and horrors. They could never understand how I had stood, dirty and tired and cold, in a potato tump and contemplated marrying Norman. What was real to me was not real to them, nor to my friend Kathleen, or even to Bill, who came on Saturday evening and treated me with more respect than he ever had before.

Everyone was bored with the war and disturbed by increasing shortages, but they were carrying on as usual. My strange excursion into the winter countryside was just a good story, nothing more.

On Sunday evening a family friend came to dinner. When she heard that I was going to Wellshalline, Mrs. Brown said, "That's by the River Severn, isn't it? North of Shrewsbury? I have a very old friend, Mary Howell, who lives near there. We were at school together and I stayed with them a few years ago. Delveney Hall is a lovely little Elizabethan manor house; really a small farm. Most of the land was sold, but they have a few fields and keep cows and hens. David Howell is something important on the Agricultural Committee and doesn't do any farming himself. They have two children, who must be grown up now. I remember the walled kitchen garden where peaches were ripening, and an old orchard. You *must* go there, Prim. I believe Mary keeps open house now that we're at war."

"Prim's sure to be lonely," said my mother.

"Jane will be near, and Hilary isn't far away," I said, for I had bought a large-scale map of the area.

"Still, Mary would take an interest in you. Give me some paper and I'll write a letter of introduction."

Mrs. Brown wrote the letter, and I took it without

realizing how important that introduction was to be, though an Elizabethan manor house with a walled garden sounded lovely. I had so longed for something beautiful, out there in the bleak Cheshire fields.

Mother came into my room that last night and said, "Prim, you look in splendid health, but are you really happy? Is it the right life for you? Your poor hands are in an awful state, and your hair hadn't been washed for weeks."

"Yes, it is the right life," I answered. "I have to do it."

The Land Woman

In the train, on my way to Chester, I took another look at my map. River Farm was marked, and so was Jane's Melwardine Farm, and they were only about two miles apart. Hilary's farm, at a place called Shawley, was a mile or two beyond Jane's. I did not know where Peter Blane lived and didn't want to find out. The River Severn wound through the countryside, and the Vyrnwy was not far away, either. Near where the two rivers met, Delveney Hall was marked.

Across the River Severn was another country, Wales. There seemed not to be a proper bridge nearer than Montford Bridge, but there *was* a railway bridge near Wellshalline, and a station was marked on the English side. But I had been told to go to Shrewsbury and then take a bus.

I met Jane at Chester General Station, and we went to Shrewsbury in an unheated, overcowded train. We were both wearing our Land Army uniforms and heavy shoes, with our big rubber boots tied onto our suitcases. As we left the train, a tall woman came up to us briskly. "I'm Mrs. Blount, the assistant regional secretary. Are you Primrose Harvey and Jane Preston? The train is very late, but we expect that nowadays. Have you had any lunch?"

Rather taken aback, for we had not expected to be met, we confessed that we had not eaten, and she led us firmly toward the refreshment room. Mrs. Blount explained that she had a committee meeting and so could not drive us to our farms, but she would take us down to the inn yard.

"It's a real country bus, girls. And I inspected your farms personally. They are both clean, and your rooms will be perfectly adequate. I'm sure you'll both be very happy."

Her brisk manner almost dared us to be happy whatever happened. A cold woman, with no nonsense about her. A drawing there somewhere? No time to think it out, as we were led, lugging those very heavy suitcases, to the inn yard, where the bus waited.

"Best of luck, girls! Work hard!" said Mrs. Blount, and departed.

We shoved our suitcases into the little old bus. It was already fairly crowded with women carrying laden market baskets. They had lilting voices that reminded me of Peter Blane's, and it was all suddenly lovely and friendly. They all took a great interest in us, and Shropshire began to seem a much softer and gentler place than our native Cheshire.

The bus left very late, because the driver was waiting for someone he knew meant to travel. In fact, he seemed to know everyone. It was a bright day, with a touch of warmth in the sun, and I felt a surge of excitement and joy because spring was coming at last. When we turned into narrow lanes, with high banks, I gave a cry as I looked ahead, where the land dropped, for there were strangely shaped hills, blue and clear, and behind them higher mountains.

"Those are the Breiddens, dear," the woman behind said over my shoulder. "Beautiful hills, aren't they? Of course they're in Wales."

In Wales; that other country that was so near. I loved North Wales, but had never seen the part we were looking at.

"Where are you going, dear?" the woman asked.

"To River Farm, Wellshalline," I told her. "The Clarks."

There was a silence. I knew other people had heard. I turned around and the woman who had asked the question had an impassive face. "The Clarks," she was murmuring. My heart sank and I whispered to Jane, "Is there something wrong with them? Oh, I do wish you were coming with me."

"I wish I were, too," Jane said. "Oh, Prim, this is really the beginning, isn't it?"

We stopped in a tiny village with charming, cream-washed cottages, and several people left the bus. There was a sign at the top of a lane: FERRY. But a woman said, "It doesn't run any more, dear. Stopped years ago."

I saw the words "Wellshalline Store and Post Office"

on a small building and cried in panic, "Shouldn't I get off?" A dozen voices answered: "Not for more than a mile yet, dear."

"I asked Mother to send my bicycle," I said to Jane. "We must meet as soon as we can. Have you got a bike?"

"Matron said I could have her old one," Jane told me. "It'll come in a day or two."

The land rose and fell gently, so different from the flatness of Westringham and Rillsden. If only Jane had been coming with me I would have been perfectly happy. I had fallen in love, from a bus, with that lovely scene.

Voices told me I must alight at the next corner and I staggered to my feet, grabbing my suitcase and flapping boots. "I'll come and look for you as soon as I can," I said to Jane.

I left the bus and it rattled away around a corner. The air was cold and very sweet and the river gleamed a few fields away. I stood still, breathing deeply. There *was* a railway bridge—maps don't lie—but it looked partly derelict. I could see great gaps between the sleepers high above the river. A strange, unsafe roadway to Wales.

But what was wrong with the Clarks? I asked myself, as I turned into a muddy lane where a tiny signpost said: RIVER FARM. The farm had been inspected and was clean. At that point, remembering Littlewood, cleanliness seemed all important.

Some way ahead was a large, plain brick house with

an extensive group of buildings behind it; clearly River Farm. The mud in the lane had been pressed up into ridges by the passing of carts and tractors, and walking was so difficult I couldn't look around me much.

There were two old cottages on the left and I stopped near them to take a rest. One looked neat and well kept, the other very tumbledown. Yet it was occupied, for some washing hung on a line, and a small girl of about four was standing behind an iron gate. She had pretty blue eyes and curly dark hair showing under an old woolen hood, but she looked very thin and pale and she had a crop of sores around her mouth. Another Dolores? Though she was basically a much prettier child with a lively, intelligent expression; not shy, either.

"Are you the Land Woman?" she asked, as I put down my suitcase.

"I suppose I am," I said. "Who are you?"

"Eileen Myfanwy Parry. I was four last week."

The way she said her middle name sounded like Mu-van-wu, but I knew how it was spelled. The f is always v in Welsh. I looked at her and smiled. "That's quite old," I said.

"My dad's down the fields. He's the waggoner at Clarks'. And my mother isn't well, and our baby has the stomach ache." Her voice held a little more than usual of the local lilt.

"Oh, dear! I'm sure they'll soon be better, though."

She eyed me interestedly. "My dad says he's sorry for the Land Woman, having to live at Clarks'."

I picked up my luggage and walked on. In fields on either side of the lane was a large motley herd of cows. Shorthorns, Friesians, two or three Ayrshires, and a number of Herefords. I counted uneasily, and there were at least eighty of them. I had been almost praying that I would be sent to a farm where I could hand-milk. Peter Blane had said he would tell the office I ought to be, but either he had forgotten or they had taken no notice of his directive. There obviously must be a machine at River Farm. And I was so stupid about using one.

I tramped up to the house, and went around to the back door. Dazzlingly white curtains hung at all the windows. The place was well kept and utterly different from Littlewood. Timidly I knocked at the door, and it was opened by a tall, rather stately woman with beautifully waved gray hair.

"I'm Primrose Harvey, the new Land Girl," I said, and she answered, "Come in. Wipe your feet well. You can unpack and by then the cows will be coming up. We milk at four-forty-five. I suppose the bus was late, as usual."

The kitchen was spotless; there couldn't have been a greater contrast to Littlewood. The stairs were covered with carpet and she made me take off my shoes, saying she hoped I would always wear slippers in the house. My room was quite large and as clean as possible, and the bathroom was next door. I caught a glimpse of pristine towels and toothbrushes in a row. On my bed lay two equally pure towels and a new cake of soap.

Mrs. Clark looked around, then eyed me carefully.

"You're very young, but you look strong and a nice type of girl. We had some evacuees, but they've gone back to Birmingham. So we thought . . . a Land Girl . . . take up one of the rooms. Our daughter is getting married soon, and that leaves far too much space."

Well, that was frank. Get the bedrooms filled so that there would be less chance of more evacuees when the war hotted up.

The room was cold, and the bright sunlight was on the other side of the house. Her presence was somehow chilling, too. A hard woman, I thought, but she'd probably be better than Mrs. Farndon. And yet I had a sudden, unreasonable longing for that other farmhouse, with a dog and a lamb by the fire, and Norman smiling his sweet, secret smile. And Jane. . . . Oh, Jane! I saw her standing in the frozen fields, playing her pipe for Norman's benefit. I longed to know what her farm was like.

I went downstairs eventually, wearing slippers and carrying my boots. A table was laid in the window of a pleasant sitting room; all very civilized. No screaming, unchanged baby, no smells, but . . . "My dad says he is sorry for the Land Woman." And Eileen Myfanwy's dad lived in that tumbledown cottage up the lane.

I put on my boots and headed for the farmyard. The

March day was turning cold and cloudy, but rooks were cawing in some high trees. The cows milled around me as I made my way to the door of the nearest shippon. Shippon . . . well, they were called cowsheds in Shropshire.

In the doorway stood a short, stocky man wearing a thick tweed suit. He had a heavy, ill-tempered face and didn't smile as I approached him. "Mr. Clark? I'm Primrose Harvey."

"Yes, the wife said you'd come. Help to tie up the cows, will you? Claud is seeing to the feed." And he indicated a very old man who was hobbling along with corn and cattle cake. The old man gave me a long look and chuckled. "Primrose! You're as welcome as the flowers in spring, my dear. But a town girl! Can you work?"

"I can work," I told him. And he winked and hissed, "You'll need to. The old man's a slave driver, but show me the farmer who isn't."

The cows were housed in four sheds, and I saw with dismay that there were five milking units and a spare. At Westringham we'd used only three and a spare, and at Littlewood Jane had used four. Five units would mean that I would have to dart anxiously from one to another, and one or two units would have to go ahead into the next cowshed. But I didn't have to cope with that on my first evening. A man called Geoff was in charge. He was the cowman and he had a lovely voice and a quiet face, and I knew I would like him. There were several other men moving quietly about, helping with the foddering and washing the udders, but their personalities were not very clear to me that day. I did notice one of them particularly, because he had a shriller voice than the others and sounded more Welsh. He had a thin face that twitched and he lost his temper with a cow, calling it something that the other men seemed to think unsuitable.

"Not before the Miss," Geoff whispered. Then he said to me, a few minutes later, "Dai Parry is a bit jumpy. Shell shocked in the other war when just a lad. Better with the wagons than with the beasts."

"Has he a little girl called Eileen Myfanwy?" I asked, and he nodded, and said, "Yes, and a boy, Rhys, eight, and a baby girl, six months old. And his wife is a very sick woman but won't see a doctor. Scared, and it costs too much. A very nice family, though."

"Welsh?" I asked, and he told me, "Not Mrs. Parry. She comes from this side. Dai, he comes from the other."

As we were nearing the end of the long milking he said to me, "You watch the old man, Miss. They're a hard pair, him and his missus. Don't like the men, but needs us, see what I mean? Sort of an enmity. It's not unusual. It's always been them and us, between the farmers and the workers. One day things will be better; maybe the war will help. We'll get a fairer wage and proper overtime . . . status."

"*I'm* a worker," I said, looking into his quiet, intelligent face.

"Yes, and he'll see he gets the last bit of work out of you. It's not right for girls. But his own daughter was never having any. Left school and got herself a job in Shrewsbury, and soon she'll be married and gone. But *we* have to get on with them. Tied cottages—come free with the job, you know—and there's Amos, the shepherd, with his smallholding; fears to lose the right to rent it if he quarrels with the old man."

"I didn't understand," I said. Them and us. The longer I was in farming the clearer it became. I was always one of the workers, on their side. And this was something they hadn't told us about at Westringham . . . they had left the politics out of it. We were to work on farms because there was a war on, but there was no indication that we might find ourselves one with underpaid, overworked, often bullied farm workers who had to put up with it all because they might lose the few benefits they had. The country scene was not in any way as I had imagined it; if it was idyllic, it was only in brief flashes.

Anyway, when we had finished milking I was told to feed and shut up the poultry, and then I hurried indoors and changed out of my uniform into a dress. Then I ate supper at the table in the sitting room with Mr. and Mrs. Clark and their daughter, Milly. The food was good, but I felt uneasy. Mr. and Mrs. Clark hardly spoke to each other, and Milly seemed in a dream. She was quite an attractive girl of twenty-one.

"Bit mad, aren't you?" she asked, when we met on

the stairs after the meal. "You wouldn't have been called up for ages. I'm getting married partly to avoid call up. If it comes I'll see I have a baby."

"Do you think they will call up all the women?" I asked, rather shocked by her attitude.

"Sure to, if the war goes on. I don't fancy being in the Services; I like an easy life. And my Harry is thirty-three and connected with agriculture."

I spent an hour or two sitting by the kitchen fire while the Clarks occupied the sitting room. I wrote to Mother, then did two drawings. One of Eileen Myfanwy inside the cottage gate, and me with my suitcase outside it: "Are you the Land Woman?" And the other was of Dai Parry cursing the cow. I began on another of Mrs. Clark saying: "You may be an outdoor worker, but don't put that filthy mud on my stairs." But I didn't finish it, because she might see the picture and be angry.

I went to bed feeling lonely and strange, missing Jane's warm body beside me. I was sure I had struck unlucky in some ways, but, however I felt about the Clarks, I had to stick River Farm and make good. And in the morning I would see the lovely hills again, beyond the shining river, and it would surely be no hardship to work in those sloping fields, with the rooks cawing and the grass beginning to grow after the bitter winter.

I Fall in Love with a House

By the time Saturday came I was certain that I had been unlucky with my farm. Apart from the horrors of that complicated milking, it was, at first, nothing really tangible, just an awful feeling that I was on the outside, tolerated but not liked, not even regarded as a person. They thought it was a good idea to have "a girl" and, having got her, that was enough. The girl was fed, her room was clean, and she was largely ignored.

Mealtimes became an agony of shyness and self-consciousness. I suppose I really wasn't old enough, or experienced enough, to cope with such a social problem. Yet I think even someone older would have been daunted. In fact, I wasn't *expected* to talk. No one talked much. At first I wondered if it was because I was there, but after a while I was sure that had nothing to do with it. I did go through agonies of misery wondering if they just didn't like me, but common sense began to tell me they would have behaved exactly the same whoever had come. There seemed almost no communication be-

tween Mr. and Mrs. Clark, and not much between them
and their own daughter. And what Geoff had said
about the men was clearly true; they were tolerated because they were needed, but the Clarks seemed to take
no interest in their lives. Mr. Clark rarely spoke at all
at meals, but if he did say anything it was usually something derogatory about them.

The men treated me with an old-fashioned respect
that I found funny, touching, and a little irritating.
They always referred to me as "the Miss." I said, "My
name's Primrose, or usually Prim." They laughed and
continued to call me Miss, and any coarse language was
hushed up in my presence, so different from Mr. Farndon, who had sworn heartily without thought of my
delicate sensibilities.

In the *place* I had struck lucky, for its beauties were
ever present during the first two days when I worked
"down the fields." The changing light over the river
and the distant hills and mountains always delighted
me, and the softening air made me happy. Apart from
milking, sterilizing the tankards and the machine, and
looking after the poultry, I did field work. The milk
was all sent away; there was no milk round. My first
day I helped Geoff, who was cutting down a thick thorn
hedge. I made great piles of wood, and we got them
burning with some difficulty. But, once they were well
alight, it was lovely. The smell was delicious, and the
columns of blue smoke blew away over the river.

"But we must make sure they're out before dark,"

Geoff said. "Daren't leave anything burning. Blackout and all that."

"There aren't any German planes," I said, unable to imagine the enemy over our quiet fields.

"There will be one day," he answered. "Anyway, it's the law."

After dark our remote countryside was as black as Wallasey had been. Blacker, because there was so little traffic. I looked forward to the lighter evenings, when I needn't sit alone in that unfriendly kitchen.

There was a lot of work to be done in the fields. Plowing, which had been held up because of the long cold spell, was now well under way. Oats would be sown and potatoes would be planted, and several fields of sugar beet. Shropshire, I learned, was to try and produce a good crop of sugar beet because there was going to be a great shortage of sugar. Muck had to be spread.

"The old man'll get you onto that," Geoff told me. "Probably tomorrow."

He was right. Dai dumped patches of muck all over one of the big upper fields and showed me how to scatter it around evenly with a fork. Then he went off to plow. Left alone, I began to work. Heave muck up . . . scatter it. After an hour I found it very boring, my only entertainment the wide view under the bright sky. I adored that view, but after two hours my back and wrists were aching and I longed for companionship. It was only eleven-thirty. Dinner wasn't until twelve-thirty. Then I saw a tiny figure plodding bravely toward me.

Eileen Myfanwy, wearing rubber boots, an old coat, and her woolen hood. "Well, hello!" I said, as she drew near.

"My dad said to come and talk to the Land Woman."

"My name's Primrose," I told her. "You can call me Prim. I'm glad you've come to talk to me."

She talked, following me from patch to patch, carefully avoiding my swinging fork. She talked well for a four year old, and quite amusingly. Chatter about her dad; her brother, Rhys; the baby, Dilys; and their cat, which had just had kittens. We walked back together at dinnertime, me carefully checking my footsteps to match her small but firm strides.

"I like you, Primrose," she said, as we reached the cottage gate.

"I like *you*, Eileen Myfanwy," I answered, smiling at her. And so began a relationship that was to grow much deeper. She was a warm and loving little girl and, I soon learned, very different from her brother, who had a shrill voice like his father's and a penchant for doing mischievous, even spiteful, things.

Later that day I met Mrs. Parry in the lane near the cottage. She must have been very pretty, but she was thin and pale, with a bad cough, and I thought she probably had tuberculosis. She was friendly and seemed sorry for me, apparently because I lived at the farm.

"Anything I can do I'll be glad to, Miss," she said.

Thursday morning there I was back in the muck field—spread, spread, spread. It was a dark morning, cold and depressing, with mist hiding the hills. I sang,

I recited poetry out loud, but not even washing flowerpots at Westringham had been as boring as spreading muck all alone. I told myself I was helping the war; that the grass would grow strong and sweet over the pasture field where I was working. That was one of the hardest lessons I had to learn; the monotony and primitiveness of many of the farming tasks.

"They ought to have a *machine* to do this," I thought savagely. And knew they probably had, at Westringham.

About eleven it started pouring rain. No one came to tell me to stop, so I kept on until dinnertime. When I returned to the house I was soaked, and Mrs. Clark viewed me with disfavor. Mr. Clark was sitting by the kitchen fire, perfectly dry. After dinner he said I had better clean out the hens and ducks, so I put on my sodden outdoor clothes again and worked all afternoon, pushing laden barrows to the midden through the awful mud and the pouring rain.

After the evening meal I arranged all my wet clothes in front of the kitchen fire, and Mrs. Clark came in and saw them.

"Well, really, Primrose, what a mess!"

"But I must get them dry!" I said, rather desperately.

"Well, hang them in the scullery."

I did, and of course they were all still wet the next morning, which was blessedly dry again with a hint of sun. I told Dai, while we were mucking out, and he said, "You bring them along to our place. One thing we always have is a good fire."

So that's how I first came to rely on the Parrys for warmth and comfort. But I was really shocked when I first entered their cottage, for the kitchen was worse than Littlewood. There was little furniture and, what there was, was broken and dirty. At first I thought the floor was just earth, until I realized that the stone flags were so muddied over they were entirely hidden. Dirty baby clothes lay around, and there were unwashed dishes piled up by the sink. *But* there was a roaring wood fire, with a kettle singing on the hob, and the warmest possible welcome. Eileen Myfanwy clung to me, and the baby smiled and waved a tiny hand. The cat lay in a basket with her kittens, and there were some pussy willows in a blue jar.

"Always bring your clothes here to be dried," Mrs. Parry said, arranging my things on an old-fashioned clotheshorse. "Won't help you, will it, if you start with rheumatism?"

She gave me a cup of strong tea, and I went "down the fields" with the knowledge that I had friends. In spite of the poverty and mismanagement, there was kindness to a stranger. But I told myself I must not accept the Parrys' hospitality without making some practical return. I could provide packets of tea, and other little gifts now and then.

By the weekend I had learned quite a lot about Wellshalline, the place where I was likely to spend the next few months, or even years. It was a very close-knit community. There were only buses into town three times a week, and most of the life of the place went on at the inn, the Severn Bank, and in the Women's Institute. Mrs. Clark belonged to the institute but, according to Geoff and Dai, wasn't popular. "But then no one likes them around here," said Dai.

I wasn't surprised but I was still very puzzled about why they were as they were. I stared at Dai and he went on, "Plain enough, isn't it? Superior, they are. Particularly Mrs. Clark. The story goes that she was a rich girl; her dad was what they call an industrialist in Birmingham. Owned factories, even got a title. She came here on holiday—had an aunt here in those days—and met Nat Clark and they fell in love. Her dad had other ideas; didn't want his daughter marrying a young farmer. So she ran away, and he cut her off without a shilling, as they say. When he died he left every penny of his money to a younger brother."

"Oh!" I found it hard to imagine cold, stiff Mrs. Clark so driven by love that she could do such a thing. "But . . . then why? . . . I don't think they love each other now."

"Didn't work out, I suppose," said Dai, and gave his shrill laugh. "Never does, does it? All right while you're young and it's exciting. After that it usually goes wrong some way, but you put up with it."

Dai with an ailing wife, and Mr. Clark with a tall,

108

handsome woman who rarely spoke. Oh, all the time I was learning, and much that I learned I didn't like.

I asked Geoff about Jane's farm and he said it was smaller than River Farm and not so well run, but the Headleys were nice people, with some nice children, and treated their workers better than most.

My bicycle had come, and I longed for Saturday afternoon and freedom. I awoke to a fine morning, but my spirits sank when, after breakfast, I received a letter from Norman. I read it standing in the muck field, as the lovely hills turned blue, and, as I read, I was back in the potato tump, hearing a gentle voice proposing marriage.

"Dear Prim"—Norman wrote in a childish hand with many misspellings—"I hope this finds you as well as it finds me. Things aren't the same here without you. The orphan boys are awful and Mrs. F. bullies them something terrible. I have joined the Army. I did it in Rillsden yesterday. I'm going into camp in the South next week. Learn to kill people and all that. If I get killed I give you all my love. Please send me a letter. Norman."

I leaned on my fork, looking across the shining river, and I felt pain and guilt and a warmth that was a kind of love. I heard Dai saying: "All right when you're young and it's exciting." I *knew* I could never have married Norman, that I had done right, as far as right was possible. But by my refusal I had sent another human being out into a world of war and fighting and

109

maybe death. And I began to scatter that muck fiercely around me, wondering where Norman would be when harvest time came and another winter. I was glad when, at ten o'clock, Eileen Myfanwy came to keep me company.

I got no money. Mr. Clark said he would pay me next week, as I had not worked a full week. He paid the men after dinner. Dai said he often delayed just out of mean mindedness until the only bus had gone into town.

After dinner alone with Mr. and Mrs. Clark (Milly was in Shrewsbury with her future husband, who had picked her up in a smart Ford) I took my map and set off to look for Jane. I needed the map because the signposts had gone; they had been taken away in case of German invasion.

It was a really heady sensation to be free, though I would have to be back for milking. The hills were dazzlingly clear and there were celandines on the high banks. I was cycling slowly along when a lorry overtook me, then stopped. A familiar voice cried, "Well, little one! We meet again!" and Hilary leaped from the driver's seat and came toward me. She was wearing a white raincoat with a scarlet scarf tucked into the neck and at first seemed a vision from the distant past.

"Jane said you weren't far away," she said. "I met her on Thursday, when I was driving past Headleys'. You'll find the child very happy. She sits in the straw and plays that whistle of hers while those great dumb beasts are milking."

"While the machine is on them?" I gasped, thinking of my own frantic rushes from one cowshed to another.

"Fantastic, isn't it?" Hilary asked. "They're already treating her like a daughter. Luck to meet you, darling child. Look, you and Jane must come and have supper with me on Monday night. I'll pick you up about seven at River Farm."

"But can you have two people to supper?" I asked blankly.

She laughed. "As many as I can fit in. My work is dead boring, and the people are boring, too. Really, I do find the country dreary; this ghastly obsession with beasts and crops. As for the Harper kids . . . the most painful little horrors, but I've made them toe the line pretty smartly. And I have one great advantage. My quarters are a small flat over the garage. I can have meals with the family, or cook my own. The only reason I sometimes endure family meals is economy. I'm writing another novel in the hope of supplementing my income."

I looked at her with some of my old awe. An actress, *and* an author. And funny, too. I could *see* those poor farm kids being kept in order by a drawling word.

"You are *lucky!*" I cried. "I manage the most awful machine, with eighty cows to milk. And the Clarks are the queerest people. It's clean, and I'm well fed, but sometimes I wonder how I'll bear it."

"Then don't, little one. Tell the office it isn't suitable and ask to be sent somewhere else."

"I can't," I said. "They might remember *I* was said to be unsuitable. I've made up my mind to stick it out for six months. Then I'll see." Until that moment I hadn't realized my mind *was* made up. I added, "Isn't it a strange coincidence that we three from Westringham have all ended up so close together?"

Hilary laughed again. "I came here by sheer chance, but I doubt if you and Jane did. Peter Blane probably had something to do with it. He's well in with the Shrewsbury office, and he knows all the farms around here. Well, I must fly. See you two children on Monday." And she climbed back into the lorry and drove away.

Peter Blane! As I rode on I was filled with hatred for him, remembering all the times he had humiliated me. He had probably got me sent to Clarks' out of sheer spite or mischief.

Jane's farmhouse was tucked into a hollow under a red sandstone cliff. It looked very old and very shabby and a million times more attractive than River Farm. Jane met me at the gate, smiling and pink cheeked, and it was all true. The Headleys were so kind, and the cows loved her pipe, and she was happy. All in six days.

Jane's room had a tipsy floor and low oak beams, and we sat on her bed and talked. Then we had tea and hot scones with the family, and I cycled back to River Farm in time for milking.

On Sundays I was free, except for milking morning and evening. Once a month I was supposed to have a whole weekend when I could go home. I had asked Jane to go with me to visit Mrs. Howell, and we met at a crossroads and rode on, into a tangle of narrower lanes, until we came to gates, a long, curving driveway, and a lovely black and white house on a slight rise, among trees.

Delveney Hall was enchanting. I fell deeply in love with it at first sight. Jane's little farmhouse had moved me because of its oldness, but this house was even more fascinating, with its uneven roof lines, twisted Tudor chimney pots, and the patterns of the half-timbering.

I dismounted halfway up the drive and stood gazing, and in that moment, somehow, everything was worthwhile. Fate, or Peter Blane, had brought me to that remote corner of Shropshire. Mrs. Brown's letter was taking me to Delveney Hall. The miseries and tension of River Farm faded away as I stood there, with the sun on my face and the rooks cawing in the high trees. Here and there a glimpse of that strange enchantment. Tomorrow muck spreading, hour after hour. Today . . . followed by Jane, I went slowly toward the house.

Peter Blane Again

"I don't think I should come in," Jane said nervously. "*You* have the introduction. She doesn't know me."

"No, but I was told she keeps open house. Don't desert me," I said urgently, for I, too, felt shy. But I longed to establish contact with the people who lived at Delveney Hall. I was putting down roots into that lovely countryside—and yet, during that first week, most of my life had been harsh reality.

And now an ancient, half-timbered manor house on an afternoon when spring was definitely in the air. A little warmth in the sun, the cawing rooks, and the first daffodils surging up the green bank below the south front of the house.

"Mrs. Brown *said* her friend keeps open house," I repeated, as we drew near the front door. One of the windows was a little open and music came pouring out; a Mozart piano concerto.

Around the side of the house came a young man. He was tall and very thin, and he wore shabby trousers and a thick sweater with a large darn in the front. He was rather nice looking; fairish, with gray eyes. He stared at us, and we stared shyly back, clutching our bicycles. We were both wearing our Land Army uniforms, so at least he knew that we were farm lasses. *He* didn't look like a farmer, even though his clothes were so shabby. He looked delicate and bookish.

"Hello!" he said.

"Hello!" I answered. "We've come to see Mrs. Howell. I have a letter of introduction from a friend of hers in Wallasey."

"Oh, Father and Mother are in the walled garden, I think. I'm Edward Howell. Let's go and look for them, shall we?"

We left our bicycles, and, as we walked beside a high wall and approached a green door, we told him our names and where we worked. He opened the door and there was the walled garden. It seemed to hold a special warmth, for every trace of wind was shut out. Fruit trees were trained flat against the old walls, and the narrow paths were bordered with tiny box hedges. The walled garden of Delveney, almost bare in the very early spring, but to be known in a glowing autumn.

Mr. and Mrs. Howell were down at the far end, where another door was open to reveal an orchard. As yet there was no blossom, but daffodils bloomed around the apple trees. Mr. Howell was a tall, craggy man in a thick tweed suit that nevertheless had a town air, and

115

Mrs. Howell wore slacks and a thick blue sweater. She was older than Hilary but she had a face like Hilary's— intelligent, bony, not pretty at all, but most interesting.

"Two lost lambs with an introduction," Edward said. He had the lilting voice of the country.

"They can't be *lost*," Mary Howell said. "Land Girls. . . . How do you do, my dears?" She read Mrs. Brown's letter and smiled warmly. "I'm glad you've come, Primrose. And this is a friend of yours? Jane. . . . Welcome, Jane. I hope you'll both come often when you have the time. I feel I must do something, so I try and welcome as many strangers as possible."

"Primrose is at Clarks' near Wellshalline, and Jane with the Headleys at Melwardine," Edward told them, and they exchanged glances.

"Clarks'?" Mr. Howell repeated, and his tone told me he knew about the Clarks. "Are you happy there, Primrose?"

Pride came to my rescue. I couldn't complain; anyway, it might get back to the Clarks. "It's very clean, and I have a nice room. But I wish I was at a handmilking place, for I was so good at that."

They walked us around the garden and the orchard, then into an old stableyard close to the house. In one of the buildings there was a great deal of noise—voices, laughter, and banging. The door was open and I saw figures in khaki.

"There's a new Army camp a mile or two away," Mrs. Howell explained. "Poor boys, it has few amenities.

116

We've given some of them that barn for their own use. They're making scenery and plan to put on a play in the village hall. Such nice lads, and most of them far from home."

There were other farm buildings at a little distance, and we went to look at the pigs and poultry, and admired twelve pedigree Friesians out in a field. In another field were three riding horses and a cart horse.

Mr. Howell's office was in Shrewsbury, and he explained that, since the outbreak of war, he had had little time for his small farm. He employed two men and a boy. One of the men was very knowledgeable and efficient. The other—Benny—was almost seventy but insisted he would die working rather than retire.

"We only have a few fields now," he said. "Just enough to grow fodder for the animals, and small crops of potatoes and sugar beet. The rest of the land was sold to Mr. Blane in my father's time."

"Blane?" I repeated, so sharply that they all looked at me. "We had someone called Peter Blane instructing us at college." I was filled with dismay. It was hard luck that Peter Blane's farm was so near.

Jane and Edward had wandered away and were deep in talk. I wondered what Jane would say when she heard.

"Oh, yes, Peter," Mrs. Howell said. "He's finishing at the college at Easter; then he'll be managing the farm. It's quite a big farm and is one of the best in these parts. A Shorthorn herd, and pedigree pigs. And his father was a keen horse breeder. You ought to go and see it one day. Poor Peter! He's had a bad time lately. Well, we'd better get back to the house as it's nearly teatime. Four o'clock."

"I have to be back for milking," I said. "Sundays we milk at five." But I was longing to see the inside of the house.

"You've time for a cup of tea and some of Hannah's hot scones. Hannah looks after us, and we're lucky to have her. She's seventy-five but as spry as if she were forty. All the local girls are joining the Forces or going into munitions. It won't take you long to cycle back." Mrs. Howell led me firmly toward the house. Edward and Jane were already waiting in the front porch, which was made of very ancient black wood. "By the way, Peter's here now. He's home for a weekend, but his mother has a sister staying with her, so he escaped to Delveney. He's playing my daughter Annice's records. Annice is a Wren, stationed near Plymouth."

It was too late to retreat. As we were led into a dark old hall, I found myself next to Jane. "Blanes' farm is next door, and Peter's here," I whispered urgently. "I didn't know until it was too late."

I had thought I would never see Peter Blane again, and I certainly didn't *want* to see him. Hilary seemed to think that we were where we were because Peter Blane had been recruiting Land Girls for North Shropshire farms. All my painful memories came flooding back.

We were led into a beautiful, shabby old drawing room with wide window alcoves. The house smelled deliciously of polish, wood smoke, and sheer oldness. But all my joy of being there was quite spoilt. Peter Blane was sprawling on a couch, listening to the last notes of a Beethoven sonata. He looked utterly at home; his arms were behind his head and his shoes were on the floor beside him.

"Two of your students from Westringham, Peter," Mrs. Howell said. "I'll just go and tell Hannah we need tea quickly, as the girls have to get back for milking."

Peter slid from the couch, thrusting his feet into the shoes. He didn't seem in the least discomposed, or even surprised. "Well! Primrose and Jane! How are you? Surviving, I hope?"

"Just about," I said, as coldly as I dared, with Edward Howell and his father listening.

"Primrose is with the Clarks near Wellshalline, and Jane with the Headleys, Melwardine," Mr. Howell said, and Peter Blane looked at me.

"The Clarks?"

At that moment Mrs. Howell and Hannah opened the door and wheeled in a tea trolley, and the next few minutes were devoted to pouring tea and handing out hot scones. Jane and Edward were sitting together on another couch, and I caught them exchanging shy, experimental glances. With a flash of awareness, I knew that they liked each other. Then I saw Peter Blane staring at me, and I met his eyes with a blank look. If I owed River Farm to him, then it was something very big against him.

All too soon, in some ways, we had to leave. Mrs. Howell said, "Do come whenever you can, girls. We'll be delighted."

We began to wheel our bicycles away from the house and were just mounting when a shout behind us made us pause. Peter Blane, now wearing an overcoat, was running to catch up.

"I'm going home, too," he said. "Look here, Primrose, what's the meaning of those frightful glares you've been giving me? Surely you've forgiven me for anything I said and did at Westringham? You've both turned out well, and I was wrong. I told you so. Remember? Are you all right with the Clarks?"

"If I'm not," I said, one foot on the pedal, "it's thanks to you, as far as I can see."

"What do you mean? Don't be a fool!"

"I suppose it amused you to see that I was sent to a place that milks eighty cows with a machine? And where they only want a girl because she fills a room, and that may mean one less evacuee."

He looked so genuinely astonished that I took my foot off the pedal.

"I told both the Chester and Shrewsbury office to send you to a hand-milking place, as you were a natural," he said slowly. "Those fool offices don't listen to anyone. As for Clarks' . . . I said all the other places should be filled first, as I didn't think a Land Girl would be happy. It's a well-run farm, and no doubt the house is well run, too. But . . . well, the Clarks are a very respectable family, though not exactly outgoing to strangers. Don't blame me, Primrose. If you're unhappy I'll deal with it when I come back after Easter."

"Don't bother," I said, though I was ready to believe him. "I've decided to stay there for six months. I can't keep on changing, can I?"

"No, but—"

"We have to get back for milking. Goodbye!" I mounted and rode away, followed by Jane. We sped down the slight hill, through the open gates, and into the narrow lanes.

"You were very sharp with him," said Jane. "And really, he seems much nicer than we thought at first."

"I daresay," I answered. "But, in spite of him, aren't you glad we went to Delveney, Jane? It's beautiful, and the Howells are so nice."

"I liked Edward," Jane said. "Do you know, he wants to join the RAF, but they won't take him. He failed the medical, and he's very much upset about it. He had an illness last year and hasn't been very strong ever since. He says he'll keep on trying until he's accepted. He works in the library in Shrewsbury, and he collects books on aviation. He's going to show them to me next time we go."

"You seemed to find plenty to talk about."

"Well, he was telling me . . . then we talked about books."

Jane had left school at fourteen, but I knew that by then she had read a great deal.

I had fallen in love with the house, and I wondered if Jane had fallen in love with Edward. There was something about her that was different; I could feel it, even cycling along so fast. After I had parted from Jane, and was rushing toward River Farm, I remembered Norman's letter and felt sad again. Love . . . what a mess! Before Norman, the only person I had ever been attracted to was Bill Wainwright and, ironically enough, he had meant very little to me that weekend I had been home.

I arrived only just in time to help tie up the cows. Milking passed smoothly, and I cooled the milk, sluiced the machines, brushed my boots, and went toward the house. Supper with the Clarks . . . six months of suppers and other meals. But, on the good side, I had got the hang of the machine and established some kind of rhythm. And there was Delveney to think about.

While we ate a delicious meal, I looked from one expressionless face to another. Milly was to be married next Saturday; then I'd be alone with Mr. and Mrs. Clark, horrid thought. Was it a horrid thought to them? Two personalities imprisoned behind those unresponsive faces. But I was probably as good as anyone else.

Six months of my life seemed a very long time. Maybe, at the end of them, I would know of some other farm nearby that wanted a Land Girl. For I didn't want to go away from the area.

A creamy pudding followed roast duck. Mrs. Clark might have been a rich girl once, but she had certainly learned to cook. I glanced covertly at her and really couldn't imagine the violence of love that had made her cut herself off from money and luxury. I wondered if such emotions always faded away. What if I had married Norman?

But, after the meal, I wrote him a long letter, as kind, warm, and amusing as I could. After that I did a drawing of Peter Blane sprawling on the couch with notes of music over his head. "I prefer this to tiresome girls who are learning farming."

It was one of the drawings I would never be able to use.

Springtime in Shropshire

Milly was married in the little church in Wellshalline, and the reception was held in the village hall. Quite a few of the local people were invited, and had accepted. I thought cynically that, in a countryside where there was very little entertainment, no one was going to miss such an affair.

I was not invited. I worked as usual on Saturday morning, spreading that boring muck in another field, and a few sandwiches and some cold apple pie had been left for my dinner.

From the field I saw her being driven along the lane, splendid in white and decked with orange blossom; a lamb to the slaughter or, rather, a lamb that would find a way *not* to be slaughtered by the call-up machine.

Mr. Clark had paid us all after morning milking; an unprecedented happening, evidently. Most of the men went off into Shrewsbury on the bus, and I went to find Jane. And, at suppertime, the Clarks and I were alone, but they actually talked to each other about the wedding.

I got to know the cows; I even gave some of them names. It was not a pedigree herd, so they didn't have names in the herd book. One day I happened to be in the cowshed alone when a cow started to calve, and I stood there fascinated, wondering if I should shout for one of the men. But old Claud came hobbling along and said, "She's an easy one. Be here in no time. Just have to see the calf doesn't have membrane over its nose. Many a good calf lost because it never starts to breathe."

It was a Friesian cow and we had a Friesian bull. The calf that fell sprawling into the world of River Farm was attractively marked in black and white and perfectly healthy and breathing. It wasn't a *pretty* sight, but it was a wonderful one . . . almost a touch of the strange enchantment on that day in spring. Another living creature to wander in the fields above the river, growing in the sun.

Easter came and I went home for the weekend. It was splendid to be "free," but somehow I couldn't really enjoy it. It was good to have meals with Mother and Charlie, but I did rather feel as if I had dropped down from the moon, thoroughly alien. Bill asked me to go to the cinema with him and I went, but what would once have been a small miracle was just a pleasant enough evening. Right in the middle of the film *Goodbye, Mr. Chips* I was wondering what Jane was doing at Delveney. Walking with Edward? Or rehearsing in the barn? For we had been roped in to act in the play and to help with costumes. It was a very ordinary play, a comedy, but it gave some of the boys from the camp an outlet and there was a certain amount of talent. The scenery was finished, and it was fun to try my hand at acting.

As the evenings had grown lighter, Jane and I hardly ever stayed alone at our farms after milking. Often we went to Delveney, or were entertained by Hilary. All fears of the dark lanes on the return journey had left us. Already we knew every twist and turn, and if we met anyone it was probably a member of the local defense volunteers going on duty to watch for invaders. The war had hotted up, but it was far away still. Most of the news was about Norway.

I went back to River Farm on Easter Monday. I only managed it because of Hilary's kindness, for I couldn't have afforded a taxi. But Hilary met me in her farm truck and took me to have supper at a pub.

"Dear child, how was the world?" she asked me, as we ate meat pie and thick bread and butter in the smoky atmosphere of the ancient building.

The world? The world of Merseyside, where the war had not yet struck. "Town doesn't seem right," I said. "I'm indoctrinated or something. The world is a few miles of North Shropshire, in fields above the river, where all those darn cows have to be brought in for milking. And hens that need feeding and mucking out, and those awful geese that always go for the seat of my breeches when I'm carrying two buckets."

"It can't stay that way, little one," Hilary answered. "It won't for me, and it won't for you. Six months at River Farm, you said."

"And then another farm. Unless the war's over."

"The war hasn't really started for us. Come on. Let's get you back. By the way," Hilary added, as we walked to the pub's car park, "how about letting me use some more drawings? The novel won't bring in any money for a long time, and I'm getting short. I must write another article. I'm sure you have plenty of pictures."

"They're not all for publication," I answered. "I don't want any more trouble. But I could do with some money, too."

"Well, let me have six or eight of your funniest, and I'll write the article around them."

She insisted on driving me up the lane to the gates of the farm. It was a clear night, with stars, and the brick box was quite visible. Strangely, now I was back, I felt myself again, though I dreaded entering that unfriendly house. I must be *mad*, I thought, as I jumped down and felt the chilly silence roll over me. No welcome, up for milking at five-thirty, back to potato planting.

The week before I went home I had done nothing but bend over the drills, dropping the potatoes evenly into holes. If not evenly, Mr. Clark, who was supervising, gave an irate yell. So primitive; at Westringham there would surely be a machine.

"By the way," Hilary said, leaning out as I walked

around the truck, "riotous amusement for you, little one. A message from Peter Blane. He wants us all, you, Jane, and me, to go to tea at Blanes' farm—it's really Welsh View Farm—next Saturday."

I forgot the stars and the cold, sweet smells. "Oh, don't be funny!" I cried. "I'm not going to tea with Mr. Blane!"

"And his mother, don't forget," Hilary drawled.

"Well, I'm not going to tea with his mother, either."

"Jane has accepted and so have I." Hilary sounded coolly amused.

"Oh, no!" I said, so loudly that the farm dog began to bark. "Tell him he can go . . . oh, tell him I'll *come*."

"I'll give him your gracious message, Prim," said Hilary.

I walked around to the back door of River Farm. It was locked, so I had to ring the bell. Mrs. Clark opened the door after such a long interval that I was beginning to think I'd have to sleep in the barn.

"We had given you up, Primrose," she said coldly.

"It's only ten o'clock. I did say I might be late."

"Well, make yourself some cocoa or something."

"Thank you. I've had supper. Good night, Mrs. Clark."

"Good night, Primrose."

In my cold room there were clean towels, and a new cake of soap. "The girl" was looked after. How much did they dislike me? I had no idea.

128

Indoors at River Farm I was deprived of companionship, even of ordinary conversation, but the rest of my life was crowded with people. Claud, Geoff, Dai, and the other men had accepted me and I liked them more and more, even Dai, who, because of his disability and troubles, was often shrilly short tempered. The Howells of Delveney . . . the boys who used the barn . . . Jane and the Headleys . . . Hilary. And Peter Blane, who somehow lurked in the background during that week after Easter.

My love of Delveney Hall had deepened with other visits. It was a darling house with its uneven floors, dark and twisting staircases, and mullioned windows. Most of all I liked the huge stone-floored kitchen where everyone was made welcome by the old woman, Hannah. There were always apples from the loft, as well as sandwiches, and soup on cold days.

I had plenty to think about during the monotonous hours in the fields, though potato planting was not a solitary job like muck spreading. Someone had to hold the other end of a box containing seed potatoes.

But, among all those people, one person stood out; one very small person who had somehow grown attached to me. Eileen Myfanwy Parry, four years old, from a ramshackle cottage where there was great trouble but as bright as a button and ready to spill a fountain of love.

She was there in the lane, waiting, when I came out

ready for field work on that Tuesday after Easter. Her hair was blowing in the mild wind and her pretty face was free of sores for once. She flung herself at me and hugged me around the hips.

"Prim! Oh, Prim! I missed you. Don't go away again."

"I shan't, for a month," I told her.

She raised her face, smiling. "No, don't. I love you. I do. You're the nicest person I ever met, yes, indeed."

"But you love your father and mother and Rhys and Dilys," I said, a little embarrassed because I had never had much to do with a very young child before.

She said, "Yes, but me mam's ill and often cross, and you're never cross, and you're so pretty. And me dad says the Clarks must be mad not to 'preciate you."

As she fell into step with me, taking exaggeratedly long strides with her tiny boots, she continued, "We went over the bridge yesterday to see Granny, me dad's mother. She gave me twopence."

"Over the bridge . . ." By then I understood the significance of that phrase. Half the families around had relations on the other side, in Wales. Much courting had been done by way of trips over that dangerous, abandoned railway bridge. People carried babies over it, and bicycles, with scant thought for the gaps between the sleepers. Jane and I hadn't ventured yet, though it was a powerful attraction—a quick way to head for the inviting hills.

"Twopence is a lot of money," I said, walking faster

because Mr. Clark was waiting in the potato field. The child ran to keep up with me.

"Yes. I wanted to give it to me mam for the doctor."

"For the doctor?"

"Doctors cost a lot, but me dad says she should see the doctor. She coughed all night."

If Mrs. Parry didn't do something soon, she would die. Maybe it was far too late already.

It was a glorious morning, with the small green leaves of the hawthorn running brilliantly over the hedgerows and the hills and mountains wreathed in light. The earth was awakening after the bitter winter. It was already April, and before we knew it May would have passed and it would be June, and time for the hay harvest. Everything would grow so fast, surging out of the earth as the sun grew warmer, and, in that dreadful little cottage where I had found a refuge, there would be tragedy. And what would happen then to Eileen Myfanwy, so brave and bold in her small rubber boots?

The child had endless spirit. The geese were nearly as big as she was but she minded them less than I did, and once, when the bull got loose in the lane, she stood her ground, saying in a loud, clear voice, "Go back, bull! *I'm* not afraid of you." And it was Dai, swinging her to safety over the cottage gate, who was sweating and shaking with fear.

I knew from our talks by the fire that Mrs. Parry had no relations and that Dai's mother was half-crippled with arthritis and lived with an old cousin in a tiny cottage. There would be no home there for Rhys, Eileen Myfanwy, and baby Dilys if their mother died, and Dai seemed to me a helpless, feckless man in the house. My troubled thoughts carried me right into the potato field, and were only dispelled when Mr. Clark demanded to know why I hadn't been quicker. He sent Eileen Myfanwy away with a few sharp words.

So there I was back in Shropshire, bent double over the damp earth, and only straightening up occasionally to get another box. The sun was quite warm, there were sweet smells, and my back had almost ceased to protest over all the bending.

I went to see Jane that evening. She was waiting for me and said we had to go to the barn for a rehearsal. "They're putting on the play in ten days' time. They've got the church hall at Delveney for two nights." Jane looked relaxed and happy though she, too, had been planting potatoes all day long.

Jane . . . my sick elf of a few months before. Edward Howell, eating out his heart because he couldn't join the RAF, had made a friend of her. I didn't want Edward, luckily, but I did want Delveney. The usual joy filled my heart as we cycled up the drive and I saw the house above me. Four hundred years of obscure history filled its rooms. Darling Delveney, smelling of polish, and age, and hyacinths in bowls.

"I wish you hadn't agreed to go to Peter Blane's," I

said, as we parked our bicycles. "*I* don't want to see him."

"I knew you wouldn't be keen," Jane said, "but it was hard to get out of, and he isn't as bad as we thought. None of it matters now, does it? We're on farms and he's left the college."

He was a farmer; a young farmer with many responsibilities. And, as it turned out, we had a very pleasant time on Saturday.

Hilary's presence took the strain off the visit. Calm, relaxed and faintly amused, she did most of the talking. After greeting me with the words, "Hello, Prim! Nice to see you again!" Peter Blane didn't notice me particularly, so I was able to give most of my attention to the new farm. Welsh View Farm was quite large, with a pedigree herd of milking cows, pigs, poultry, and a few sheep. Winter wheat was already green in two large fields, and others were planted with oats, potatoes, and sugar beet. Running free in a field above the river were some fine horses and three gorgeous foals. Peter watched them, frowning.

"Horses were my father's beloved sideline. He had quite a reputation, but I doubt if I'll be able to keep it up if the war goes on for long. Most of them will be sold eventually."

The farmhouse was another old building, part half-timbered and part red sandstone, and its main rooms had views over the fields to the Severn and the Vyrnwy, and the hills of Wales.

The two big surprises were how different Peter Blane seemed at home from the irritable, sarcastic young man of Westringham College and his mother. Though I knew he was only twenty-five I had vaguely expected someone elderly, but she was only forty-four (she told us quite soon that she had had Peter when she was nineteen), and she was good looking, smartly dressed, and pleasant enough, though rather embarrassingly dramatic, I thought, over the untimely death of her husband. Clearly she made her son uneasy and I began to see why he had escaped to Delveney.

It was such a lovely day that we had tea outdoors in a sheltered corner, and I ate scones and cake dreamily, gazing at the view and then up at the old rooflines of the house. After several days in the potato fields it was luxury to sit in the sun and be waited on.

Hilary did no milking so she was in no hurry to leave. Mrs. Blane was talking to Jane as we went toward our bicycles, and Peter walked by my side.

"Prim, are you really all right at Clarks'?" he asked.

"Yes, I have to be," I said. "I mean to stay until September, unless they chuck me out. By then most of the harvest will be in, and we may know what's going to happen to the war." But, oh, how far away war seemed on the April afternoon, with a glimpse of apple and plum blossom in the orchard. The whole countryside was drowning in blossom.

"We'll know," Peter said grimly. "Look here, Prim, you have forgiven me? I know I was a sarcastic brute

134

to you, but all those women at Westringham did get me down, and I thought you were out to be funny."

"If you think it *funny* to be buried in pig muck, with some of the porkers on top of you . . ."

"No, I don't. It was horrible for you, and I ought to have had more sense. As for drawings, you showed great talent. Have you done any more?"

"About three dozen," I told him. "I've just given Hilary some more, for her new article. Every time something happens I see it as a picture. Yesterday old Claud, who mostly fodders the cows and mucks out, came to help with the potato planting, and at the end of the afternoon he couldn't straighten up. It *wasn't* funny, he must have been in agony, but he said, 'How'm I to lie in me coffin all bent up like this?' And, later, I did a drawing of him in his coffin all arched up, and I called it 'Blame the potato planting. Me back never straightened after that.' "

He laughed, but said, "You're an uncomfortable young woman to have around. I don't know what the Clarks make of you."

"They don't know or bother. I hide my drawings carefully."

"Well, to show you forgive me, will you come to the dance at Melwardine next Wednesday? Tell the Clarks you'll be late back. I'll pick you up at seven-thirty."

"But . . ."

"It'll be a riot. Half the Army will be there. There's another camp beyond Shawley. But I'll look after you."

"Well, I suppose so," I said, astonished by the invitation.

"And there's another thing. Can you ride?"

"No-o. I've stuck on horses now and then. At Littlewood I sometimes rode the pony up the fields, when the snow was going."

"I could teach you. Some of those horses of mine need exercising."

"Without sarcasm?" I asked. I longed to be able to ride well.

"My tongue shall be buttoned up," he said solemnly.

"You'd better ask Edward to take you to the dance in Melwardine," I said to Jane, as we cycled through the lanes, but she said, "I don't think he'd care for it."

On Wednesday evening the Clarks gave me a key with obvious reluctance. They never actually said anything but I knew they disliked my growing friendships in the district. Even if I hadn't told them myself, dropping occasional remarks into the silence of a meal, someone else would have done so. Nothing remained a secret for long.

Peter picked me up in his shabby old Ford and we found the village hall at Melwardine already crowded with soldiers and a few civilians. There was a terrible dearth of women, and Peter didn't manage to dance with me all the time. Because of the blackout regulations there was no hope of getting much air into the hall and the atmosphere was soon stifling. We danced and sang and stamped on the floor, and it actually bent during the Palais Glide; there was an awful slope in the middle. But it was the greatest fun, and I saw another side of the irritable Mr. Blane of Westringham. Sweating, laughing, dancing as hard as anyone, he looked years younger. He took me back to Clarks' at midnight, and I tiptoed upstairs in my stockinged feet, tired and happy.

"The Germans Have Entered Paris!"

May came and by the tenth the hawthorn was in full flower. I felt as if I had been in Shropshire forever. Delveney was a second home, and Welsh View Farm on the way to being a third. At first I had been shy with Peter's mother, but she was really quite nice and made me welcome for tea on the two Saturday afternoons I went to the farm for a riding lesson. Peter was a fine rider and a good teacher, and I felt confident from the first. He was never once sarcastic, and he taught me to ride on a horse that was quieter than most.

All over that countryside I knew people; I belonged. But Hilary, who had nearly finished her novel, said she wasn't planning to stay much longer. She would go back to London and try to get a part in a play.

"Children dear, I can't stagnate in these bucolic fields forever. My views have changed. Like the London Blonde, I find I'd sooner die in a place where I belong."

"But you belong here. You were born in Shrewsbury," I argued.

"A long, long time ago, dear Prim. My own kind are in London."

"Don't leave us!" I cried, for I still found her amusing, and something more than that. "And why *should* you die in London?"

"People are going to," she said. But in all that glory of spring, with hawthorn, lilac, and laburnum everywhere, and the oats and wheat growing in the fields, not to mention potatoes and sugar beet, the possibility of death by bombing seemed remote.

And then, on May 10, the war storm burst over Western Europe. There were German air raids on towns in Holland and Belgium, and German forces crossed the frontiers of both countries. Many German soldiers landed by parachute near harbors and airfields. The Dutch and Belgian governments appealed to Britain for aid, and, when I heard the radio news in the old drawing room at Delveney that evening, I was suddenly afraid, for the war had come much nearer. Mr. Chamberlain, the Prime Minister, tendered his resignation to the King, and the Whitsun holiday was canceled.

Edward Howell walked with Jane in the walled garden, no doubt pouring out his frustration at not being allowed to join the RAF, and Mary Howell said to me, "This is the real beginning, Prim. And it may be very wrong of me, but I pray that Edward will remain exempt."

A day or two later there was a letter from Charlie.

He said he'd finish his year at the university and then join the RAF. He sounded wildly elated, but fear stabbed at my heart again. Those heavenly May evenings were almost unbearably beautiful while so much horror was going on in Europe.

There was always somewhere to go. Once a week, Jane and I had supper with Hilary. She talked increasingly of going away. "I can't stand those rotten little kids at the farm much longer," was her way of putting it.

My skin was tanned, my hair dry after so much sun, my hands raw and occasionally bleeding. As the days grew very long we worked longer hours and milked later. Geoff said that, when haymaking time came, we might be working to get the crop in at nine o'clock at night. "And no overtime, either," he said, "unless the old man's in a very good mood." There was no protection for farm workers.

"Things'll be better one day," Geoff said. "They have to be."

"Under the Germans?" old Claud asked sourly.

"*Not* under the Germans. When we've won, I mean."

Hot sun and flowers and working until one almost dropped, but there was still energy left for the evening's amusement. Peter and I went to another dance, at Shawley, and danced until nearly midnight, and twice he drove me into Shrewsbury to see a film. I had grown at ease with him, and liked him very much, but there was no real intimacy. He never kissed me, nor even held my hand, but he seemed to enjoy my company.

The retreat of the British forces, struggling desperately toward Dunkirk . . . the saga of the rescue from the beaches by the little ships sent out from English ports. . . . During those days I could think of little else, as I hoed potatoes and sugar beet hour after hour, hot and desperately thirsty. Norman might be there on the French coast. He had written to me twice from France. I saw him dying on the sand and remembered his sweet smile. *Was* it my fault if he were there?

In Wellshalline, there was a hint of tragedy. Rhys Parry was run over by an Army lorry and was taken to hospital, but he turned out not to be seriously injured, and his mother grew thinner every day. She struggled on, saying that the hot weather got her down, and no one dared to tell Dai that his wife was dying. Dai was so excitable it was not a good idea to upset him, but, watching helplessly, I wished I had the courage to tackle him.

Dai was even more excitable as May became June and the war news grew worse. "Got to beat the Germans!" he would yell. Dai hated the Germans, which was not surprising, as that other war had turned a healthy young man into a nervous, often shaky middle-aged one.

Through it all Eileen Myfanwy remained the firm and loving little character she had seemed at first, marching over the summer fields in broken sandals instead of rubber boots. I feared for Eileen Myfanwy, so warm and loving, but could only watch and wait.

Suddenly, at the end of the first week of June, haymaking was upon us. The pale gold fields waved in the summer breeze, and the hedgerows were starred with wild roses and fragrant with honeysuckle. White elder flowers were everywhere. Oh, far, far in the past were those rainbow-hued, icy dawns, when our noses froze and so did the little ducks' water bowls. On Friday, June 7, we heard that there had been air raid warnings in twelve English counties and some bombs had been dropped, but all Mr. Clark seemed to care about was making plans for work in the hayfields on Monday.

Haymaking was hard work—shaking, turning the haycocks after a sudden shower, then heaving great forkfuls up to the men on the wagons, hour after hour in the hot sun. We worked again after milking, in the cooler air. Jane, at Headleys', wasn't worked half as hard. When I managed to cycle over to see her late on the Thursday evening, she said she sometimes sat on top of a load and piped the wagon back to the farmyard.

And all the time the battles raged in France, and the Germans drew nearer to Paris. I had been to Paris with the school the summer I was fifteen and I remembered it vividly. It seemed impossible that an enemy army could ever walk the beautiful streets of the city.

But on June 14, when I was returning to the hayfield after midday dinner, Geoff burst out of his cottage and shouted to me, "Just heard it on the radio! The Germans have entered Paris!"

June 15 was a Saturday. Mr. Clark wanted us to work in the afternoon, but the men refused. They had had very little overtime money, and I had had none at all. We had worked until ten o'clock the previous evening; then I'd had to shut up the hens and geese.

"Hay'll keep until Monday, Boss," Geoff said quietly, standing up to Mr. Clark for once.

Conscience told me we ought to work until we actually dropped, whether or not it was Saturday, but I was thankful for the freedom. Since the terrible news that Paris had fallen I had been secretly sick with fear. Were we going to lose the war, then?

After dinner I cycled through the burning hot lanes to Jane, whom I found sitting on the farm gate, with her bicycle against the hedge, waiting for me. Nearby was Hilary's lorry, and Hilary herself was standing looking up at Jane.

"So, little one," she was saying, as I pulled up in a cloud of dust, "this is goodbye. It's back to reality for Hilary Buckden."

"Isn't this reality?" I asked, in a panic. "Oh, Hilary, don't go! We'll need people we know. You can't go back to London to get killed."

Hilary surveyed me coolly, and suddenly I was conscious that I had paid very little attention to my appearance. I had dragged on a clean cotton dress, washed my face and hands, and flown in search of Jane. Hilary was beautifully turned out; she was wearing a dark blue dress with white collar and belt, sheer stockings, and smart shoes, and had taken a lot of trouble with her face. Her sallow skin was deeply suntanned, and the bright light showed up every line on her face, but she looked . . . the way I could never look, in a million years. With the Germans in Paris, and air raids over Eastern England, Hilary Buckden was in command of herself.

"Whether or not I get killed is in the lap of the gods, Prim, my dear," she said. "I'm going back to London on Monday. If the theatres stay open maybe I'll act, if I'm lucky. Maybe I'll drive an ambulance, or join the WAAF or the ATS. We will see, but go I must."

"But farm workers are so much needed," I gasped. "The hay harvest is almost in, but everything else is growing. Britain may only survive if . . ."

"She won't listen," said Jane. Jane was as brown skinned as a gypsy, with bright eyes and rosy cheeks, and she wore a crisp yellow dress. I looked from her to Hilary. They had no one to worry about; Hilary seemed to have no attachments, and Edward Howell was safe at home.

I was full of fear for Charlie, and for Bill, who was joining up also. Norman might already be dead, and, coward that I evidently was, I seemed afraid of everything.

"So goodbye, kiddies," Hilary said. "I'll write and tell you what happens, and maybe we'll meet again some day. We'll have a reunion if the war is ever over. City streets are my place, and I should have known it last autumn. Never mind, put it down to experience. It'll make a good book one day; a book, anyway. And you do more with those drawings of yours, Prim. That second lot got a lot of praise."

Yes, they had, in a Birmingham newspaper. I had done my latest picture at eleven o'clock the night before. A drooping Land Girl, me, trying to heave up an over-large forkful of hay. "Paris has fallen and I'll be the next. My back is breaking." Sometimes I wondered where my ideas came from. All my thoughts of Paris were romantic and painful, yet that wretched funny drawing had been born.

Hilary drove away and Jane and I went to Delveney. In the walled garden there was the hot, acrid smell of the box hedges, and unripe peaches clung to the sun-warmed bricks. Edward Howell was sprawled on a seat in the orchard, and he obviously cheered up at the sight of Jane. Those two were growing very friendly indeed. I thought they were in love, though Jane had not said a word to confirm it.

I wandered back through the walled garden, pausing to breathe deeply of all the wonderful scents, then crossed the stableyard and entered the house by the kitchen door. The kitchen was cool and shadowy and there was no one there. I sat on the big, well-scrubbed table and tried to think. War . . . Paris . . . air raids . . . enchanting summer, glorious with roses and tall

145

grasses . . . a house that had stood for four hundred years. Suddenly I began to cry and couldn't stop.

Mary Howell found me there, with my face drowned in tears. She was often a very brisk woman, but it seemed she could be tender. She pulled me from the table and hugged me.

"What is it, Prim? Something at that awful farm of yours?"

"No. No. I can't get things sorted out. Paris and the war, and yet so beautiful and peaceful here. And Hilary's going back to London on Monday."

"I can't get things sorted out myself," she said. "Edward gets harder to live with every day because he's been turned down again, and yet I can't be anything but thankful. It does seem wrong to be in so much peace, but you are doing a good job. Isn't that enough?"

"Yes, I suppose it ought to be," I agreed, sniffing. "I don't want to go away from here. I love it so, though of course I hate living at River Farm. But all the rest makes up . . ."

"Of course it does. Help me to get the tea. Hannah's gone out. Aren't there any boys in the barn today? It's very quiet. There's a new lot at the camp. I do so hate to see them go away."

So I helped her to get the tea ready and we all ate it in the cool drawing room, where tall vases were filled with many-colored lupins. And, gradually, the horrifying visions of the German columns moving into Paris retreated a little. Hope began to come back. The war was not lost; the Germans would never conquer London. And my job was clear; hard work all summer. I still couldn't think of Charlie, or of Hilary going away on Monday.

The Fate of Eileen Myfanwy

"It was inevitable, though, you know," Peter Blane said to me, when the hay was all in and I was free again in the evenings. He had come in his car and taken me for a drive over Montford Bridge into Wales. Petrol was getting scarce, but he had an allowance as a farmer and just occasionally his conscience allowed him a short pleasure trip. We were sitting on a little hill, among poppies and moon daisies, looking toward the higher hills. "Hilary is a strange kind of bird, and certainly a city one. I never knew how she got hold of the mad idea of joining the Land Army. Or why *you* did," he added, shooting an odd sideways glance at me.

"I've turned out all right," I said. "And no thanks to you. There isn't a girl works harder in the whole countryside."

"Yes, I know. You work *too* hard. There are supposed to be regulations about a forty-eight hour week."

"Don't make me laugh!"

"I won't. I know it's impossible to stick to that. But in September you're going somewhere else."

"Yes, though the evil one knows is better than the evil one doesn't know, I suppose. I've grown used to not talking in the house, and I still dry my things at Parrys', even though . . ."

"She's bad, I hear," Peter said gravely.

"Very bad. I don't think it can go on much longer. She struggles to cook, and wash a few clothes and look after the baby. Rhys is back home and worse than ever. He's not a nice kid; he's the kind who goes around pinching and throwing stones, and teasing animals if he gets the chance. Eileen Myfanwy is a kind of miracle. She gets brighter every day. The things she says . . . and life's going to explode in her face."

"You love that child?"

"I guess I do," I said sadly. "But I'm not going to be able to help her when the time comes."

"You may," Peter said, and slewed around among the daisies. "Prim, come kiss me. One ought to kiss on a hillside in summer."

I was startled, though really I shouldn't have been. We had got to know each other pretty well by then. He was burned brown by the sun and it made him look very attractive. He was smiling down at me, as I lay among the flowers. Kissing *was* right in summer.

We kissed. It was rather more than nice, and it ended too soon for me. He stopped rather abruptly and stood up. The sun was sinking behind the mountains and it was growing cool and dewy.

"Must get you home," he said, and took my hand

and drew me down the hillside. Driving back to the bridge he was unusually silent; then suddenly he fired at me, "How old are you, Primrose?"

I gasped and opened my mouth to say, "Nineteen in January." I said, instead, "Seventeen."

I saw his hands tighten on the wheel and he gave a loud whistle. "Good heavens! Am I baby snatching? You're joking?"

"No, I'm not," I said. "I told a lie when I joined the Land Army and put a year on my age. I was only sixteen then. But my mother knew; she agreed. After all, I was tall and strong, and war had been declared. I had my seventeenth birthday at the college."

His face was rather grim. "And I bullied you. You're a brave girl, Primrose Harvey, but I wish you were older. Why, I must seem like your father."

"Not at twenty-five, and not when you were kissing me," I said. "I feel heaps older than I am. Can't you just forget it?"

"I don't know," he answered, and we drove in silence to River Farm.

All through the rest of June and during July the war news was worse and there were air raids in different parts of Britain. We even heard the terrible sound of enemy planes over our quiet corner of Shropshire and a few bombs were dropped in Wales. I went home for a weekend early in July, and Charlie had already joined up and was to be off in a week or two. Mother was calm and apparently resigned, and I felt guilty and very unhappy about her.

"Would you like me to come home and keep you company?"

"No," Mother said emphatically. "I'll be busy. I'm an air raid warden now, you know. You get that harvest in."

"I never thought you'd stick it," said Charlie.

"Did I seem so weak?" I asked sharply, wanting to cry. Charlie still seemed to think it all a joke, an adventure, but the RAF was not the safest place to be. Sometimes I hated the war so violently I felt sick. Yet, if there had been no war, I would still be at school.

In July we began to "pick" the early potatoes, so it was again endless hours in the fields, bent almost double in the hot sun or the summer rain, picking up the outflung spuds. And, meanwhile, the oats, wheat, and a field or two of barley grew ever higher, so that many of the fields above the river varied from palest silver-gold to a rich dark yellow. I often envied Jane because of her friendly, casual farm, but her fields had no view.

One day in late July Eileen Myfanwy sat on a gate, thin brown legs dangling, and asked, "Is my mother dying, Prim?" Eileen Myfanwy knew all about birth and death, living on a farm.

"Who said?" I temporized.

"I heard Geoff's wife saying so, so I asked Rhys, but he only spat at me."

"She has a bad cough. She ought to see a doctor," I

said. Next day Mrs. Parry was at the cottage gate and she said to me, "Eileen says you think I should see the doctor, but doctors can do nothing for me, Primrose." She had stopped calling me Miss.

It was very hot; thundery. There was sweat on her white forehead, and sweat on mine, too, as we eyed each other. It was a sort of nightmare, realizing she knew she was dying. *Dying*! Leaving helpless Dai with Rhys, Eileen Myfanwy, and baby Dilys, not a year old.

"But if you go to the doctor now . . ." I began, and she gave me an old, sad look, shook her head, and walked back into the cottage.

Two days later, when I was on my way back to the fields after breakfast, Dai came rushing out of the cottage shouting, "The missus has collapsed! Get the doctor! Someone do something!"

Geoff's wife heard the noise from their cottage next door and went into the Parrys'. I shouted, "I'll telephone from the farm!"

"Mrs. Parry!" I gasped, for once unafraid of Mrs. Clark's displeasure. "May I telephone for the doctor? Dr. Drew at Shawley, isn't it?"

"Really, Primrose, you are supposed to be on your way to work."

Ignoring her, I looked at the list of local telephone numbers kept by the phone and asked the operator for Dr. Drew's number. The doctor had not left on his rounds and I explained as carefully as I could.

Then, with a muttered apology, I walked past Mrs.

Clark and out into the sunshine again. So much summer beauty, so much corn growing high in the fields and the hills cloudy in the thundery air, and a once pretty woman, who was desperately needed, dying in a squalid, almost derelict cottage because of fear and lack of money.

We saw the doctor's car from the field, and, an hour later, an ambulance turned up the narrow lane. After it had driven away, Dai came slowly to work. His face was dead white and he was shaking. "Taken her to the hospital, they have."

"But what will happen to the children?" I asked Geoff, in an agony of fear for Eileen Myfanwy, and he shook his head. "The wife'll do what she can for the present, but she isn't strong herself."

The Clarks remained aloof from the tragedy at Parrys', but everyone else did what they could to help. I did my best, though I knew very little about household matters, and I was so appalled by conditions in the cottage that I was more helpless than I would have been otherwise. I had only ever seen the kitchen, but the other room downstairs was pretty well empty and the two bedrooms upstairs were unspeakable.

I knew I would never forget the horror of the Parrys' condition. A lot of it was fecklessness and mismanagement, for Geoff's cottage was not like that, but some of it could certainly be blamed on the pitifully small wage of a farm worker and on a kind of hopelessness. The others managed because they were healthy, and because the men grew their own vegetables and kept a few hens, and Amos had his smallholding. My last romantic ideas of country life died forever when I saw those bedrooms.

Eileen Myfanwy clung to me during those days. "Is me mam going to come back, Prim? Me dad's not much good at cooking. Mrs. Geoff has our Dilys. Is she going to keep her?"

I knew that Mrs. Geoff couldn't keep the baby for long; Geoff, kindly man though he was, wouldn't let her. Dai went to the hospital, five miles away, on his bicycle, and came back shrill and glum. "Ferry bad she iss! That head nurse, or whoever she is, talked to me. Dying, she said. Doctor gives her two weeks." He didn't trouble to keep his voice down so that Rhys and Eileen Myfanwy wouldn't hear. In any case, they had to know.

I told Peter and he said, "Not your responsibility really, Prim. It's the Clarks who should help."

"They keep out of it," I said bitterly. "But *I* can't, Peter, because of Eileen Myfanwy."

I told Mary Howell, and her ready pity showed instantly. "Those poor children! What is the father going to do?"

"Dai? He can't cope. I don't know what he'll do," I said.

We began to get in the harvest. The oats were ready first, on a hot day in the second week in August. My job was to take up the outflung sheaves and form them into a stock. The straw was terribly scratchy and my hands and bare arms were soon very painful. The reaper and binder went around the field, driven by Dai, and more and more sheaves were flung out, sprawling, on the short stubble. The sun burned down on my uncovered head and my inner arms bled, because I had to hold each sheaf in a certain way, to get them in place. The next day I wore a long-sleeved blouse and gloves.

One field of oats was "set up," then a second. If the weather held we would start carting and stacking. Then the barley . . . and the wheat. The harvest I had dreamed of during those icy winter days.

Mrs. Parry died before the second field was set up, and Dai had a few hours off for the funeral. It took Dai's last penny to get his wife buried. Next day some kind of social worker came to the cottage, and later I heard that she said she could get Dilys into a babies' home, and Rhys into an orphanage for boys. At the moment there was no place for a girl, but she would do what she could.

I was working until late in the evening getting in the oats. I was tired, and too hot, with torn and bleeding hands. Wearing gloves hadn't been successful in that weather. I was sick at heart for Eileen Myfanwy. On the Friday, Rhys and Dilys were taken away, and Eileen Myfanwy followed me around when she could, and for once was almost silent. Four years old and quite clever enough to know that it was the moment of reckoning.

On the Saturday, Mrs. Howell asked about the Parrys and I told her about Eileen Myfanwy's plight. She said, "I spoke to my husband about her. He heard there was no place for her. The father seems a hopeless case, and she can't be left with him. We'll take her here for a time. Maybe you'll explain to Dai Parry and bring her tomorrow? If he marries again he can have her back, otherwise we'll try and get her into a good orphanage presently."

"You'll have her at Delveney?" I looked at Mary Howell in wild relief, almost crying. Eileen Myfanwy living in that beautiful house, playing in the stableyard, climbing trees in the orchard, being given buttered crusts by kind Hannah. Clean and cared for and safe.

"We haven't any evacuees, after all, though they may come now the real bombing is starting. And you've made me interested in the child, talking about her all summer."

The bombing had more than started. It was especially terrifying to me because bombs had fallen on Birkenhead and Wallasey and, in Wallasey a few days earlier, four people had been killed.

I went to see Dai after milking that evening. He was sitting by the empty firegrate, smoking a rank pipe. Eileen Myfanwy was in bed. He didn't ask many questions, or seem surprised, but he was a little grateful.

"It's ferry good of Mrs. Howell. I wass always hearing Mrs. Howell was a good woman." He always grew more Welsh in times of stress. "Fancy our Eileen living at Delveney Hall!"

"Just for a time," I said. "Until we see what's going

to happen. Afterward maybe a children's home; she said a good one. The Howells have influence."

"Our Eileen's a bright girl. You'll thank Mrs. Howell for me, Miss?"

"Of course." I was shocked, even though I knew the difficulties, that he could let his children go so easily. "But wouldn't you like to see her? Take Eileen Myfanwy there yourself?"

But he shook his head. "Me go to Delveney Hall? No, you take her, Miss. Take her bits of clothes, too. Indeed I may not stay at Clarks' now. I'll find another job."

"But," I said, "she is your own daughter. Don't you . . . ?" And then I stopped, because I had to accept that Dai, in his present state, *didn't* care all that much that Eileen Myfanwy was going away from him, maybe forever. That warm-hearted little girl, who was strangely trusting in spite of the way life had treated her so far.

I crept up the creaking stairs and saw her asleep on top of a dirty blanket; it was a very hot evening. But she wasn't quite asleep, for she murmured, "Prim!" and spunded contented. Oh, God, she trusted *me*! Of all the things that had happened to me since I joined the Land Army, this was, in some ways, the worst and the best. Agonies of responsibility I didn't know how to handle, and the love of a four year old, when I had never had a little sister. But she felt more like my own child.

I took Eileen Myfanwy to Delveney on the seat of my

bicycle, with her "bits of clothes" in a paper shopping bag hanging on the handlebars. Jane met us at a cross-roads and dismounted to walk beside us. The child looked at her quite happily and said, "Prim's taking me to live in a lovely place. You see, me dad can't look after me with me mam gone."

So much trust. I felt a little sick as we walked along the hot and dusty lane, with the little arm around my shoulders. But I must be doing the right thing.

"Edward's trying again next week," Jane told me, and her voice sounded strained. I looked at her quickly, forgetting Eileen Myfanwy. And I asked for the very first time, "Do you love him?" And she nodded and answered, "Yes. Funny, isn't it? *Me* and Edward How-ell. I don't belong in his world."

"The past doesn't matter," I said. "You must belong. He thinks so. Well, doesn't he love you, too?"

She nodded again. "He says so, but . . . but really he cares about *nothing* but being a fighter pilot, and I *hate* the war and I . . . am afraid."

We looked at each other gravely and came to the gates of Delveney. Eileen Myfanwy gazed at the house as we went slowly up the driveway. "It's a pretty house! Me dad said it was a great, grand house, but I like it. When I'm here will you stay with me?"

"I can't," I said. "I have to stay at Clarks'. But I'll see you often."

We parked our bicycles and Edward came out of the stableyard and took Jane away. I took Eileen Myfanwy into the house by way of the front porch and the dark, cool, sweet-smelling hall, and Mary Howell was waiting for us in the drawing room.

"And this is Eileen Myfanwy Parry? Hello, my dear."

Eileen Myfanwy was never shy or awkward. She said with complete assurance, "Hello, Mrs. Howell. I'm coming to live with you, aren't I?" And she looked the long way up to Mary Howell's weather-beaten face and gave the sweetest smile.

"Her head's alive," Hannah said to me in a low voice, thirty minutes later, when she had bathed the child, and washed her hair, and put her into a torn pink dress that was clean because Mrs. Geoff had washed it. "And her body is covered with flea bites."

"I know," I said. "I'm sorry. She can't help it."

The old woman gave me a warm, comforting look. "I'll deal with her head. It can happen in the best of families, let alone in a neglected child. I well remember when Edward went to the village school. . . . But I think I'll *boil* all her clothes. I can't put them in the incinerator until we find her some more."

"I'll try and buy her a new dress next time I go to Shrewsbury."

"Oh, don't worry," Hannah said. "What she needs is feeding up."

"She's *clever*," I told her eagerly. "Do you know, she can almost read. I don't know how she learned, but she has."

Eileen Myfanwy was to have a little gabled room next

door to where Hannah slept. It smelled coolly of polish and the pink roses someone had put in a blue vase. Oh, darling Delveney, so old and quiet, that welcomed soldiers, Land Girls, and little children in need.

We all met for tea in the drawing room. Peter walked in as first cups were poured, and Eileen Myfanwy was introduced to him. She took little notice of Edward but gradually sidled to Peter's knee. She sank down beside him, clutching her mug of milk in one hand and a sandwich in the other.

"Prim's child," said Mary Howell.

"She's too young to have a child," Peter said brusquely.

"She's got this one, all the same," said Mrs. Howell.

I was due back at Clarks' for milking. There was thankfulness in my heart because the four year old who had last night slept in a filthy bed was safe and likely to be happy. She said, "Wish you wouldn't go, Prim, but me dad says Mr. Clark's a slave driver. When will you come back?"

"Soon as I can," I answered. Jane and I rode away through the summer afternoon, a Sunday in August when the world was exploding not far away, and left Eileen Myfanwy eating a sponge cake on the floor at Peter Blane's feet.

And the next day *my* world exploded. Everything happened at once.

I Am Offered a New Job

The first thing that happened on that Monday morning was that I was sent a copy of *The Shropshire Weekly* through the post. It arrived just as I was rising from the breakfast table and I rushed upstairs to my room. Weeks ago I had sent the editor a short article and ten of my funniest pictures and, since then, I had heard nothing. And now here was the current issue, with the wonderful words on the front cover: "Farming Can Be Funny, by Primrose Harvey. See Page Ten."

Pages ten, eleven, and twelve were covered with my drawings, with my article cramped in the middle of page ten. But all my captions were there in quite large-print. The drawings looked marvelous; I could hardly believe they were *my* pictures. Among them were the one of Eileen Myfanwy and me ("Are you the Land Woman?") and the one of Claud in his coffin. One of the best, I thought, was the one of me muck-spreading, with the unmistakable Breiddens in the background, and the caption: "I never want to see muck again, but I love my view."

"Primrose! Mr. Clark says hurry to the field!"

I came to myself and thrust the magazine under my mattress. The Clarks didn't take *The Shropshire Weekly*, but now that the miracle had happened and I had got my pictures into print all on my own, I was suddenly conscious that, if they found out, I wouldn't be very popular. I felt my popularity always hung in the balance. And, among the drawings, was one that was clearly of Mr. Clark, urging on a troop of potato pickers with the words: "Backs may break and you won't get a penny of overtime, but I want my crop in."

Oh, heavens, what had I done? But maybe no one would tell the Clarks, and it *was* wonderful . . . I'd surely get paid quite well. I might even be able to buy Eileen Myfanwy new dresses and pink and blue hair ribbons. I was still thinking of Eileen Myfanwy, and wondering how she was getting on at Delveney, as I rushed through the hot morning to the harvest field, where Dai was starting to cut the barley. Barley . . . no one had told me it was even more devilish than oats, that the thin spines got into every crevice, as chaff had done at Westringham, and stuck to sweaty socks and hair.

The barley field was near the road. A long time later I heard a motor bike come along from Wellshalline and turn up the lane to the farm. A few minutes later it came back and stopped by the field gate. A young man was opening the gate, a soldier with red hair. I had a sheaf of barley under each arm. I dropped them and ran. I forgot Mr. Clark, Dai, Geoff, and the other men. I stumbled on the new stubble and flung myself at that thin figure in khaki; Norman, whom I had thought might have died on the beaches of Dunkirk.

"Where have you come from? I thought . . . *Norman*!"

He looked different, so much thinner and older, but his expression was still strangely sweet, his voice gentle.

"Prim! I had to come and look for you. Went to the farm . . . some woman said you were in the harvest field. Very disapproving. Worse than Mrs. Farndon. I was in hospital in the South, then was sent to a camp twenty miles south of Shrewsbury. I'm going overseas again, so I borrowed the bike and . . ."

"But what *happened* to you?" I almost shouted.

"I was at Dunkirk and got away wounded, but I'm all right now and they're sending me off in a day or two. Don't know where. More foreign parts." He gave a funny little grin. "Oh, you wouldn't believe all I've learned since I was a lad at Farndons'. Prim, you're much prettier than I thought. Girls always look different in summer. This your boss? He's going to kill you . . . and me."

"Oh, never mind him," I said, watching Mr. Clark approaching. All those months I had felt guilty about Norman, and afraid for him, and, now that he was here, just for an hour or two I had to be free. Harvest or no harvest, war or no war. Or just *because* there was a war and Norman was going overseas again.

163

Mr. Clark came plodding stockily over the shining silver stubble. At the other end of the field, Dai was erratically swinging the reaper and binder around a corner. Mr. Clark's bare arms were red and his face was even redder.

I looked at him calmly and said, "This is an old friend who is going overseas again. In thirty minutes it will be dinnertime so, if you don't mind, I'll go off now and we'll get something to eat at the inn in Wellshalline. I'll be back at the right time, I promise."

He stopped, swallowed, and went redder than ever. "I'll dock the time off your pay."

"Well, that would be rather mean," I said, "as you owe me a whole summer's overtime, Mr. Clark. Come on, Norman," and I pushed him through the gate. I got on the pillion and we drove off.

"He'll fire you!" Norman yelled.

"Let him!" I shouted into his ear. "I only gave myself six months at River Farm, anyway, and they will soon be up."

The inn in Wellshalline was covered with pink roses. It was four hundred years old and the bar was dark and cool, with old oak tables and settles. I had been there with Peter and knew the landlord's wife. "We're hungry," I told her. "Can you manage some lunch? This is an old friend, just here for an hour or two."

"Sandwiches," she said. "Some nice ham. And apple pie and cream to follow." I nodded and ordered beer for Norman and lemonade for myself.

We sat in a dark, cool corner and ate and drank and talked. I heard a little about the nightmare of Dunkirk, but mostly he wanted to hear my experiences. Looking at his thin face in the shadows, seeing his crisp red hair, Littlewood Farm came back again from what seemed the distant past. I saw him on the cart, while I stood on the potato tump in the cold March light. Then I realized what he was saying. "Prim, I had to tell you, I wanted to see you once more. I wished it could be you, but I could see it wasn't on. I've got a girl; she nursed me after Dunkirk. She's a farmer's daughter from Kent. If the war's ever over we'll get married. Maybe we even will on my next leave."

"I'm glad," I said slowly. "I'm very glad, Norman." I *was* glad, but I remembered the terrible war news, the air battles raging over Britain, and I wondered what hope there was for any of us.

He took me back to the harvest field. It was still the dinner hour and we sat under the hedge and said goodbye. I gave him my home address, as I might not be at Clarks' much longer.

"I'm not much good at letter writing, Prim," he said, and kissed me on the cheek. Then he roared away, and, slowly and sadly, I began to set up sheaves until I heard the men coming back. Inevitably they teased me about my boyfriend, and Mr. Clark was ill tempered all afternoon. I was tired, and too hot, and longing to get away to Delveney to see how Eileen Myfanwy was faring.

Bathed and tidy, I sat down to supper with Mr. and

Mrs. Clark, and there was certainly much more tension than usual. I had erred; erred very badly. But in how many ways?

We ate cold chicken and salad in almost total silence, then a light lemon sponge pudding, which was delicious, but it stuck in my throat. Then finally Mrs. Clark poured coffee. Sipping her coffee, she spoke, "We had a special meeting of the Women's Institute this afternoon, Primrose. To arrange about the flower show."

"That was nice," I said inanely, watching her turn to the writing desk in the corner. From the top she whipped a copy of *The Shropshire Weekly*.

"Someone gave me *this*. I was extremely mortified that you had left me to find out through a fellow member. This disgraceful . . . these drawings under your name. So many people recognizable. We could have you up for slander."

"I think it's libel," I said. "In writing, though I don't know about pictures." I was babbling. I was scared.

"In such appallingly bad taste. I thought you were a well brought up girl, for all your faults. Making a laughingstock of all of us."

"Oh, hold on!" I said. "I'm sorry if one or two of the drawings aren't kind, but I'll get paid for them. Far better pay than I receive for a week of endless work in the fields." I looked at her cold face and added, "They were meant to be funny." But I knew I *had* erred in including the one of Mr. Clark.

"Hardly amusing to us," she said. "And, furthermore, I also heard, not through Dai Parry, who might have had the goodness to inform us, that you . . . *you* took his daughter to Delveney Hall yesterday to live with the Howells. You, a chit of a girl, a Land Girl, interfering in local matters. Bringing in the Howells. Words fail me!"

Words suddenly didn't fail me. "I took Eileen Myfanwy to Delveney because there was nothing else to do," I cried. "You didn't help, or offer any advice, and you knew how it was with Mrs. Parry dead. I was only thinking of the child."

"At the end of the month you can go," Mr. Clark said. "I'll write to the office."

I gazed back at him calmly. "All right. I'll write to the office, too, Mr. Clark."

I left my coffee and walked out into the hot, still evening. It was already after eight o'clock. I rode to Delveney and found Eileen Myfanwy sound asleep in the cool, oak-beamed room, where the pink roses were now full open. I kissed her, but she didn't stir.

"She's a wonderful little child," Mary Howell said. "She's followed Hannah and me around all day, talking all the time. And she's talked mostly about Prim. But what is it, my dear? You look beat."

So I told her my long tale and showed her the copy of the magazine, and Mr. Howell and Edward were there before the end and laughed over my pictures. Even Mr. Howell laughed quite heartily; then his face grew grave.

"All the same, it *was* unwise to include that one of Mr. Clark. You can't wonder they are annoyed. But since you are leaving, it leaves us free to say . . . our farm boy is eighteen and he intends to join the Army almost at once. So we'll rate a Land Girl here to take his place. How would you like the job, Primrose? You wouldn't be nearly so hard worked as at River Farm. There isn't a lot of field work. You love the walled garden. You could even work there in any spare time."

It had been a long, upsetting day and I was very tired and depressed. Mr. Howell had never seemed as approachable as his wife. But now he was smiling at me.

Slowly his meaning sank in. He was asking me to live and work at Delveney. *Delveney!*

"You can't mean it!" I said.

"Oh, he does, Prim," said Mary Howell. "We'd love to have you, and you could help with Eileen Myfanwy. She'd be thrilled."

"But would there be enough work? Is it a real job?"

"Quite real," she said briskly. "The only thing is that we won't slave drive you the way they did at Clarks'. We'll arrange it officially through the office, never fear. You'll milk, and see to the animals and the poultry and pack eggs. We send quite a lot away. And pick apples and pears and other fruit. What we don't need for our own use will all go to market. And it will be such a help having you living here. It looks as if we may soon have evacuees from Birmingham. How about it, Prim?"

I looked at the beautiful old room, with the windows

open to the sweet-smelling summer dusk, and it seemed like a lovely dream after the months at River Farm.

"I'd like it better than anything," I said.

"Let's go and walk in the garden," Mary Howell said, and she and I went through the green door into the walled garden, a truly enchanted place on that August evening. The smell of the box hedges was strong, and there were beds of phlox and fragrant tobacco plant. The peaches were ripening, and a huge asparagus bed was like a sea of pale green mist. Mary Howell looked at the asparagus thoughtfully, and said, "It's thick with weeds. You could get right under the fronds on a hot day, Prim, and weed. Oh, it will be so nice to have you!"

Jane had gone out with the Headleys, but I'd been thinking of her. I so much wanted to live at Delveney, but it was really her place. I said slowly, "I do want to come, but what about Jane? It ought to be her, because she and Edward . . ."

Mary Howell stopped her slow pacing of the narrow paths and said gravely, "I thought of Jane, Prim. But, in the first place, she's happy with the Headleys, and I don't believe she'd want to change. But I thought I ought to ask Edward his intentions, as they say. Jane is a dear girl, and I'm very fond of her. She's right for Edward. But he only wants to go to war. He's much better now and I'm afraid he'll be accepted by the RAF next time he tries. He says he loves Jane but doesn't think it would be right to make plans."

Edward, such a quiet person, but so determined to

get himself killed. "It's very hard on Jane," I said.

"Yes," she agreed gravely. "The way things are, his chances of survival when he gets flying are very slight. We have to face that."

We walked through the other door into the orchard. My feelings were a mixture of joy in the enchanted summer evening and sorrow for my friend. And other things; Norman going overseas again . . . the bombing of Merseyside and the safety of my mother . . . Charlie and Bill, training in the South. Oh, the horrors of war!

"So you'll come at the end of the month, Prim?"

"Yes, I'll come," I answered.

A Place Too Peaceful?

The next evening I told Jane about the job at Delveney. "I've said I'll go, but I hope you don't mind?"

She shook her head. "No, I'll stay at Headleys'. Mrs. Howell scares me a bit, and Mr. Howell more so. And Eileen Myfanwy is your job."

"But . . ."

"If you're thinking of Edward," Jane said clearly, "he'll be going away. I don't think there's any doubt now."

"I'm so sorry," I said. Though it was quite late we were walking our bicycles through the lanes to Delveney.

"Well, it's war, isn't it?" she said drearily. "Look at Norman, going overseas again. What are his chances of surviving and marrying his farmer's daughter? If he does survive he struck lucky there, didn't he? He'll get a farm of his own some day."

"I don't suppose he ever thought of that."

"Why not?" she said. "Norman's a bit simple, in a way, but shrewd enough. And farming's probably in his blood forever now. Maybe it's in all of us, too, just because we joined the Land Army."

"Oh, I don't see that," I argued.

"*You* may be a famous artist"—they took *The Shropshire Weekly* at Headleys'—"but I believe I'll stay in the country. Have you had any news from Hilary?"

"Yes, there was a letter this morning. She's driving an ambulance in South London, and she's got a part in a radio play."

"She always scared me," Jane said slowly. "But I liked her."

When we got to Delveney, Edward took Jane away, and Peter Blane was there. We sat in the orchard and he said, "So you're coming here, Prim. I'm glad. I hated your being at Clarks'."

"The Clarks are most displeased," I said. "Mrs. Clark, in particular, hates the idea of Delveney. I suppose she can't forget that she might have been rich and important. She gave up everything for love, and look where it landed her."

He sat with a long, suntanned arm along the back of the seat behind my shoulders. Since that evening when he had kissed me over in Wales he had seemed a little remote, though we had met as often as usual. "It will be nice to have you so near."

"Will it?" I asked, and he didn't answer, but looked at me sideways. Finally he said, "I heard a red-haired soldier turned up to see you."

Nothing could remain secret in the countryside. "Yes,

Norman," I said. "He's going overseas again. He was wounded at Dunkirk. He asked me to marry him back in March, at Littlewood." I didn't know what made me say it. I looked defiantly at Peter.

"I like his cheek!" he said, with astonishing violence. If I had wanted a reaction I had got one.

"It wasn't cheek. He's a very nice person." We were interrupted by Mary Howell calling, "Prim! Eileen Myfanwy is awake and wants to see you. And supper's ready."

I ran through the walled garden and the stableyard and in at the back door into the old kitchen. Eileen Myfanwy was standing outside her room. She looked so clean and nice in a tiny pair of pink pajamas that had been found for her somewhere. I gathered her up in my arms and put her back to bed and asked, "Do you like being here?" And she snuggled against me and answered, "Yes, I do, Prim. Ferry much indeed." Occasionally she sounded Welsh. "Do you know what? Today I hid and Hannah couldn't find me. And I ate three apples and got stomach ache. They weren't ripe."

"Well, silly you!" I said.

"An' you're coming to live here," she said contentedly, already growing sleepy again. I kissed her, put the thin sheet over her, and went down to supper. It was already almost dark. Now it was past the middle of August the nights were drawing in, in spite of double summertime, and it was getting pretty late.

We sat in the great drawing room without lights, so

that we could keep the windows open. There was just enough twilight to see what we were eating. Then Jane and I cycled through the dark lanes, parting at our usual crossroads. The Clarks had left the back door open, accepting now that I would be out until at least eleven.

My last weeks at River Farm were uncomfortable but filled with the hard work of getting in the barley and setting up the wheat. The war news was worse. Air battles raged over Southern England, and there were heavy raids on many Northern cities. I was home for a weekend during a raid and, strangely, was less scared than I had thought I would be. There was a fatalistic quality about the experience. An air raid shelter had been built in our garden in Manor Road, and Mother and I spent part of a night in it.

"I'm so glad you're in a safe place, Prim," Mother said, and I felt guilty. But I went back to my last days at Clarks', and left without regret, though I had so much liked all the men. Dai was leaving at the same time. He was going to another farm five miles away, and had been given a tiny, very ancient cottage.

"Don't you want to go to see Eileen Myfanwy, and talk to the Howells about her?" I asked him, on that last Saturday morning.

He shook his head. "What's the use, Miss? I can't take the kid, and they know what's right. If they get tired of her they're influential enough to get her into a home."

Peter Blane came in his farm lorry to take me to Delveney; my luggage and my bicycle. My room was in the narrow old passage near Hannah and Eileen Myfanwy, and there was a tall blue vase filled with goldenrod and Michaelmas daisies. Goldenrod! It was a whole year since I had listened to that broadcast telling us we were at war with Germany.

Going to Delveney to live was really like a dream, a moment of such pleasure that I could hardly bear it. For I wondered if it was really right to settle down in such a beautiful place, and do the one thing in the world I wanted, when other people were having their lives torn apart. Eileen Myfanwy was dancing around in the hall to welcome me. I had bought her two new dresses, some hair ribbons, and several pairs of white socks, and she was wearing the yellow dress, with green ribbon holding back her hair. "Prim has come! Prim has come!" she chanted.

Yes, Prim had arrived at Delveney on a golden afternoon. All over Shropshire, maybe all over England, even under those skies where the air battles raged, the harvest had almost been gathered in. The important harvest of 1940, that might help to keep Britain going during 1941. At *least* I had done that, and I felt I could eat without guilt during the unimaginable future.

I slept that night under a sixteenth-century roof, in

a place that I loved, and only awoke once to hear the distant, dreaded throbbing of German bombers going home after a raid on a Northern town or city.

At six o'clock on Sunday morning I was at my window, looking out through the leaves of a chestnut tree to the stableyard and the curves and angles of the old buildings, where swallows flashed in and out under the eaves.

Hannah was already up and gave me a cup of tea and some bread and butter; then I went out to help to bring in the cows and fodder and hand-milk them. They were splendid beasts and were giving a good milk yield, so Delveney sent a quantity of milk away. I worked with the old man, Benny Owen, who plodded quietly around, milking a few, and stripping after me. It was lovely to hand-milk again in the peace of the Delveney cowshed, to cool the milk in the old dairy, and to see Benny wheel the tankards away to the back gate, where they would be collected even though it was Sunday.

Long before we had finished, Eileen Myfanwy was with us, wearing one of her old dresses, very carefully mended by Hannah, for the new dresses had to be kept for best. Eileen Myfanwy sat on a bale of straw and talked, or chased the black kittens that were roving in the yard outside.

Then Eileen Myfanwy and I sat at the kitchen table with Hannah and ate bacon and egg and toast and homemade raspberry jam, and I was amused to see how firm Hannah was with the child, correcting her table manners and curbing her natural excitement. It was all so different from my meals at River Farm.

I had been told not to regard life as any kind of hurry, once the milk was outside to be collected, and to take an hour for breakfast every day. But I didn't need an hour, not with the lovely sun outdoors and no terrible pressure.

I was soon back in the cowshed helping Benny to muck out; then I fed the hens and ducks, collected the eggs, and fed and mucked out the pigs. The hens were laying well and some of the eggs were sent away. There was a little room where the packing was done, and I washed and boxed several dozen, helped by Eileen Myfanwy, who was very neat fingered.

After that I could have been free until afternoon milking, but I longed to work quietly in the walled garden. I weeded the paths and hoed the vegetables; then, as the morning grew really hot, I crawled under the asparagus, drawing a big basket after me. It was a strange green world and Eileen Myfanwy found it attractive, too. There Mary Howell found us when she came to call us for our elevenses. She scolded me for working on a Sunday morning.

"Can't you find anything nicer to do, Prim? Go and ride with Peter, or ride one of our own horses? I hear you're pretty good now."

"But I love working in the garden," I said.

As we walked back to the house, Mary Howell told

me that they were getting evacuees from Birmingham any day. "Two mothers, Prim, one with two children and the other with three. And this time I expect they'll stay. Last time, a year ago, our evacuees soon went back home, because nothing was happening. The children will all go to the village school, and I'm arranging for Eileen Myfanwy to go, too. She isn't five but I think they'll take her. She's bright and she'll enjoy it. And, I've been thinking, when does your mother go back to school?"

"Not until September 23," I told her.

"Then telephone her tonight and ask her to come and stay for a week. She ought to see where you are and meet everyone. Us, and Jane, and Peter Blane."

"Why Peter?" I asked, and she laughed.

"He's a friend, isn't he? He'd like to meet your mother. He told me so."

"It's awfully nice of you," I said, deeply relieved, for I was troubled about my mother, alone in the Wallasey house.

Peter telephoned after lunch to ask if I'd like to go riding with him. We rode through narrow lanes and over fields to a tiny, remote, half-timbered church on the riverbank. It was an idyllic spot; the black and white building nestled among trees, and the riverbank was cool with lush grass and flowers. We tethered the horses and sat for a while, gazing down at the water. Peter was rather silent, and I wondered why he had asked me to go out if he didn't want to talk to me.

178

"Mary Howell says I can ask my mother to stay for a week," I told him, and he answered, "Good! You'll be glad to get her out of Wallasey."

"Mary Howell says you told her you want to meet Mother. Why?"

He laughed then. "Prim, as far as we're concerned, you came out of nowhere. We haven't seen anyone of yours. You know all about us."

"I'm quite respectable," I said, a little nettled, for it didn't seem a very satisfactory answer. But he only jumped to his feet and began to untie the horses. "We have to get back for milking," he said.

As I sat peacefully milking late that afternoon I was happy enough, and yet, somewhere in my mind, there was an unsettled feeling. *Was* it right that I should be in such a peaceful place when the war was growing worse every day? But there was something else. Something had clouded that gentle dream day. Even by the end of milking I wasn't really sure what it was.

The Result of Flood Waters

September and October passed. The evacuees, very
difficult at first, had settled down, though the older
children were bored with the country and often asked
their mothers if they could go back to town. Eileen Myfanwy loved school and could soon read quite fluently.
She had filled out and was very pretty, and she walked
Delveney as if she owned it. She was amusing with the
city children; she seemed to think them quite mad because they knew nothing about the country and were
scared of the animals.

"'Course they'll go home one day," she said. "Larry
and Joan want to go *now*. Isn't it silly of them to want
to go away from Delveney?" And she sat back on the
little couch in the drawing room, with her small legs
stuck straight out in front of her, and smiled around
at all of us. Jane and Peter were there for tea.

Suddenly I couldn't look at her trusting little face, or
at Mary Howell, because, one day, Eileen Myfanwy
would have to go away, too. If her father married again,
and wanted her, there was no doubt he had the right

to take her back. Otherwise she would probably go to an orphanage; nothing had been said to the contrary.

I cycled over one evening to see Dai in his two-roomed cottage. It had ancient cross beams and an untidy thatched roof, and he was living alone in squalor. He seemed quite uninterested in his three scattered children. He was shriller and shakier than ever and was certainly quite unable to deal with a young child. The problem went around in my mind as I cycled back. While the evacuees were at Delveney another small girl made no difference, but the longer Eileen Myfanwy stayed with the Howells the worse it was going to be for her later.

Suddenly it was winter. The lovely autumn colors faded, and the fruit was all sold or stored. It rained and rained and the two rivers rose. Once I had dealt with the animals and poultry, packed the eggs, and done odd jobs around the buildings, there was not much else for me to do. On the few fine days Benny and I sometimes went hedging, and we whitewashed the cowshed and dairy. Secretly I was scared because I had had no glimpses of that strange enchantment for quite a long time. I still loved Delveney, especially on dark, chilly evenings when we had roaring wood fires, but in my heart I was unsettled and not too happy and wasn't altogether sure why. Of course the war news was awful, and there were heavy raids. Maybe I should make a decision and join the Wrens or the WAAF. But the very thought made me more unhappy. I didn't *want* to go away. I couldn't easily leave Eileen Myfanwy, who counted on me to be there. And spring would come again, far away as it seemed in November, and the crops and harvest of 1941 were going to be as desperately important as those of 1940.

Then came the day of the floods. The rivers had been rising alarmingly, and it rained heavily in the night. I awoke to a sunny morning, though, and, after all our other jobs were done, Benny said, "Let you and me go and finish that hedge in the upper field, Prim."

The upper field gave us a fairly wide view and we were watching as the rivers gave a sudden heave and overflowed. A great surge of shining water enveloped the lower fields . . . the fields of Peter's farm. Only where the land rose here and there were islands, rapidly diminishing. And on one of the islands were horses . . . but Peter would *never* have put the horses down there, when there had been danger of flooding for days.

"Look at Peter's horses!" I screamed and set off at a rapid, bumpy run. I was wearing rubber boots and the ground was uneven and sodden, but I climbed gates and stiles and arrived gasping in an upper field of Welsh View Farm. Peter and some of his men had seen what I had seen and came running.

"The gates are open!" Peter yelled. "Those blasted evacuees! That Larry and the other big boy are always going down to the river through my land. I saw them pass just before dark yesterday, but . . . we've got to get the horses out before it gets any deeper. But don't you come, Prim."

Nothing would have kept me back. I followed the men over the first two fields; then, meeting the flood water, they began to scramble along a bank. The bank, narrow and slippery, led directly to the lessening island where Peter's fine horses were marooned and getting scared. Some had been sold, but he still had ten or so, and they were very valuable. Besides, they couldn't drown. I knew those horses now.

At the end of the bank I paused for a breathless few seconds, and suddenly it was back, that old enchantment. Wild clouds had come over the sun, but still some gleams of golden light lit the rising water and the shining, terrified bodies of the horses. The scene had a nightmarish beauty. But I only looked briefly; then I found myself near the horse I knew best, a chestnut with a white flash called Star. He was looking straight at me. I always carried sugar lumps or biscuits in my pocket; messy, but useful. I spoke gently and held out my hand. At the other side of the island Peter and his men were making a great deal of noise, trying to drive the horses through the shallowest part of the flood. Star was shivering but quiet, and, miraculously, he delicately took a lump of sugar. I grabbed his mane and jumped. Even more miraculously, for I was no great horsewoman, I landed on his back. He snorted and heaved and tried to throw me. I gripped with my knees, held onto his thick mane, and said in his ear, "Go on, Star! Go *on*." And I tried to turn his head in the right direction.

One horse had gone through the flood and was already on safe ground. Star followed; luckily the water only came up to his belly. I clung on, hearing shouts behind me. Another horse floundered past. We were almost there . . . we were going to make it. But then I lost my grip and fell off, only into a couple of feet of water, but I was very wet. When I picked myself up and waded to dry land all the horses were coming over. Peter was riding one of them, but jumped off near me. He was red faced and *furious.*

"Prim, you idiot! You might have been killed! Bareback . . . you're not a circus rider. God save me from foolish women!"

Wet and cold and angry, too, I faced him.

"Well, you needn't be rude! I saved Star and I *wasn't* killed, was I? And all your horses are safe. You might have *looked* at the gates before you put them out this morning. And now I'm going back to get changed."

"The Miss was very brave," one of Peter's men said.

"Don't be a fool, Prim!" Peter said. He was still angry. "Come up to the house and borrow some of my mother's clothes. She's gone to Shrewsbury, but I'll show you her room. Do you want to get pneumonia? The wind's cold."

There was sense in what he said. Silently I followed him into the farmhouse and up the stairs. He grabbed some towels out of a chest and pushed them into my arms.

"This is Mother's room. Rub yourself down well. See if you can find some underclothes and slacks and a sweater."

184

"They won't fit me . . ."

"Well, try!" he snapped and turned to go downstairs. "I'll make some coffee."

Subdued by then, though still angry, I took off my wet clothes and rubbed myself fiercely. It felt rather awful to root among Mrs. Blane's clothes but I found a few things that would do. The slacks were too short and the sweater too tight, but I was dry and warm. Luckily Mrs. Blane had big feet, and a pair of sandals fitted me. Within ten minutes I went slowly down to the kitchen.

Peter, pouring coffee, grinned when he saw me. He seemed to have recovered his temper, but I wasn't sure I had.

"Well, you look like a daisy, Prim! Here, drink this and come near the fire. Dump all those wet things. You can have them back later. I'll lend you an old raincoat to go home."

"Very big of you," I said, and drank some of the coffee, glaring at him over the large cup. "Maybe I was silly, but I didn't stop to think, and you needn't be so rude. You always treat me as if I were a baby. And I'm *not*. I feel a million years old."

"But only seventeen," he said. "Put down that coffee before you spill it." He was suddenly very close to me. "Prim, I'm going to do a mad thing, but your mother might agree, if you do. She liked me, I think. Prim, marry me. Next summer, if you like, when you're eighteen. Or I'll wait, but promise to marry me. You love this part of the country, and you love farming. You could still do your drawing. When the war's over you could study in Shrewsbury, though I'm not sure you've much to learn. Prim, I know we started badly, and I know I haven't always been good tempered. I've known I loved you ever since that evening among the daisies, and I've told myself I was mad, but the feeling wouldn't go away. It was hard to stay quiet and not kiss you again."

He had gone on talking, while I stood and looked at him. I leaned against the old scrubbed table and was conscious of my heart beating wildly. I suddenly knew that it wasn't a surprise. There had been something for a long time; strange tensions whenever we met. And I had found myself thinking of him more and more, and wishing . . . I hadn't been quite sure what.

He kissed me. It wasn't like that other kiss on the Welsh hillside. We clung together, and in the end it was I who drew back.

"What about *your* mother?" I asked, to gain time.

"Mother's thinking of marrying again. A farmer, a widower, over beyond Shawley. But that isn't why. There was a girl once, but she went away, and now there's only you in my heart. Prim . . ."

"I think I must love you," I said. "Something happened, that night on the hill. But . . . but . . ."

"We could take Eileen Myfanwy," he said eagerly. "You adore that little kid. We'd adopt her legally, if her father would agree."

Oh, that was too much! A terrible bribe. Suddenly I wanted to get away and think; back to Delveney. To stay in that lovely countryside, to have Peter *and* Eileen Myfanwy. That could be my real war work!—bringing up a child and being a farmer's wife. But . . .

"I *am* too young," I said, and I was shaking. "It mightn't last, Peter. What then? Remember the Clarks. You'd be bored with me, because you think of me as a child."

"No, I *wouldn't* be bored!" he shouted. "Blast it, girl, you aren't a boring person. Rather an alarming one, with that sense of humor. The question is, could you marry a simple farmer?"

"You aren't a simple farmer," I shouted back. "You were a college lecturer. You've been to college yourself."

"Well, that's in the past." He was still shouting, but suddenly stopped. We stared at each other, aghast. Then we began to laugh, and ended in each other's arms again.

"Drink your coffee and go home," Peter said, much more calmly. "I must say it's a splendid preview of married life, yelling at each other. But I mean it. I love you."

"Yes." I drank the rest of the coffee and ravenously ate several biscuits. "Look . . . give me until the spring. Say the end of March. We don't know what will have happened to the war by then."

"It won't be over," he said grimly. "Tell your mother, Prim. Yes, I'll wait until the spring. Or longer. There'll be no one else."

"But you need a wife. Why should you wait?"

"And who, in this countryside, do you think I'll find?" he asked, with some of the sarcasm I had experienced at Westringham.

"Well, other Land Girls, or farmer's daughters."

"Go home!" he said. "But come back often."

Now it is the fourth week in March, 1941. I wrote this during the long, dark winter evenings, mainly in the kitchen at Delveney.

A week or two ago Wallasey was devastated by German bombs, or rather they were sea mines, meant for the River Mersey, but a strong wind blew them onto the town. Our Manor Road house was badly damaged, but Mother was on duty and so was safe. She managed to salvage most of our furniture and possessions and moved to a temporary flat. St. Helen's was bombed to the ground, and Miss Barlow was injured. I hope Mother will try to get a new teaching job in Shrewsbury or Whitchurch or some town not too far away from here. We only have each other now.

Charlie is dead. He became a bomber pilot and was shot down over Germany two months ago. I can't bear to write any more about that.

Edward is safe for the rest of the war, barring being killed in a raid. He has been given a clerical job at an RAF station in the Midlands. He crashed on an early training flight and will always be lame. He seems to me a very withdrawn and unhappy person, but he and Jane are to be married in May. They are to have a charming cottage in Delveney village, owned by the Howells, and for a time, at least, Jane will live there alone, though Edward will be with her all he can, for leaves and short weekends. Headleys are getting a new Land Girl, but Jane says she will still work for them at busy times. I hope she will be happy, but it seems so sad that Edward is still very young and Jane only nineteen, and yet somehow it is all soured already.

Eileen Myfanwy is top of her class, knocking spots off all the other children of her age. She still clings to me, convinced that she belongs to Prim first of all. She has seen her father once or twice, but he seems to mean very little to her. Dai is shriller than ever and in bad health.

Peter . . . we have been meeting all winter and getting to know each other better. All winter I have struggled with my problems and my desires. To go away to the war or to stay in Shropshire and be a farmer's wife. I might live to be eighty, more than sixty years away. In what kind of world will I live? In what kind of world will my children be born and Eileen Myfanwy grow up? It is unthinkable that the Germans will win the war, but they are bashing us terribly now.

I think I will stay. That strange enchantment that was born at Westringham, in uncertainty and dreadful cold, flashes out occasionally, strengthened by the roots that I have put down, though there hasn't been much joy these last two months, with Charlie gone and the awful happenings in Wallasey.

At Welsh View Farm I can still work outdoors when I want to, and I'll have Peter and Eileen Myfanwy. Yesterday I said to her, as we picked daffodils for the house, "If I went away from Delveney, would you like to live with me?" She was wearing a blue coat Hannah had made out of an old one of Mary Howell's, and a blue knitted cap. Her face was very different from the little thin one, with sores, of a year ago. She looked up at me and smiled, clutching daffodils.

"Live with you, Prim? Yes, please."

And I felt a sudden stab of fear in case her father wouldn't let her go, legally and forever. Of course Dai hasn't been asked yet, and he could refuse. I have heard of cases when the parents want a child back when it reaches the age of fourteen and can earn.

Mother wants me to marry Peter but thinks I would be mad to start my married life with a child of five. But if I marry Peter, Eileen Myfanwy must come, too.

"Are you the Land Woman?" How long ago that seems. The other day I came face to face with Mrs. Clark in Wellshalline. She looked at me coldly and said "Good morning!" as if I were almost a stranger and not someone who had lived with them for six months. She seemed much older and not very well. They have six evacuees at River Farm.

Westringham, Littlewood, and River Farm, then darling Delveney, and roots creeping out to Welsh View Farm all winter. All right, I'll be Peter's wife. But I'll keep on drawing; I have had several successes during the winter.

I did a drawing yesterday of Peter carrying me over the threshold of Welsh View Farm, with the caption: "If you want to keep on farming, do it as my wife."

I haven't shown it to him yet.

About the Author

MABEL ESTHER ALLAN decided she was going to be a writer when she was eight and sold her first short story at nineteen. Many years later she sold a book, the first of over one hundred she has written for young people. Except for the war years when she served in the Women's Land Army and did some teaching, Miss Allan has been a full-time author. She lives now in Heswall, Merseyside, England, where she works in a room overlooking the hills of Wales.

Miss Allan is fond of traveling and often draws the backgrounds for her books from places she has visited. Her interests also include the theatre, ballet, photography, and, very specially, folk customs and folk music.